A FATAL FORTUNE

The fortune-teller looked deep into her crystal ball as she rocked back and forth. "You want to know your future, Jessica Wakefield? I will tell you your future."

Jessica leaned forward, transfixed by Mademoiselle Z's glittering eyes.

"You will have no future, Jessica Wakefield."

Jessica gulped. "What do you mean?"

"I mean what I said. *You will have no future—unless you stay away from this carnival!*"

Jessica's heart seemed to jump into her throat. She leaped to her feet so suddenly that her knee slammed into Mademoiselle Z's table. Jessica watched in horror as the crystal ball toppled from the table and rolled across the floor.

"Out! Out!" Mademoiselle Z shouted. "And if you value your life, you will never return!"

Bantam Skylark Books in the SWEET VALLEY TWINS AND FRIENDS series
Ask your bookseller for the books you have missed

Sweet Valley Twins and Friends Super Editions

Sweet Valley Twins and Friends Super Chiller Editions

SWEET VALLEY TWINS AND FRIENDS
◇ SUPER CHILLER ◇

The Carnival Ghost

Written by
Jamie Suzanne

Created by
FRANCINE PASCAL

A BANTAM SKYLARK BOOK
NEW YORK · TORONTO · LONDON · SYDNEY · AUCKLAND

RL 4, 008–012

THE CARNIVAL GHOST
A Bantam Skylark Book / December 1990

The Carnival Ghost

One

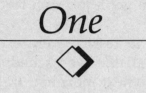

"I wish I could see into the future," Jessica Wakefield said as she watched a waiter present a plate of fortune cookies to a family seated at a nearby table.

Jessica and her family were having lunch at the Red Dragon, a Chinese restaurant at the Valley Mall.

"*I* can tell the future," Elizabeth, Jessica's twin sister, said confidently.

"Really?" Mr. Wakefield asked, smiling broadly. "When did you acquire this new talent?"

"Just now." Elizabeth winked at her twin. "Watch." She closed her eyes and put her fingers on her temples. "I predict," Elizabeth said in a low, eerie voice, "that tomorrow morning Steven

Wakefield will eat leftover Chinese food for breakfast!''

The Wakefields laughed, including fourteen-year-old Steven, who was used to being teased about his huge appetite.

"Very impressive, Elizabeth," said her brother. "Maybe you can get a job as a fortune teller with the carnival."

Elizabeth and Jessica were excited about the traveling carnival that was scheduled to open in Sweet Valley the next morning. In fact, it couldn't have come to town at a more perfect time. Christmas was over, and the carnival would give them something fun to look forward to for the remaining ten days of winter break.

"I wonder if the carnival will have a *real* fortune teller?" Jessica asked.

"I don't know, Jess, but I heard they have an awesome roller coaster," Steven answered.

"They're supposed to have a really scary haunted house, too," Elizabeth added excitedly.

Their discussion was interrupted by a smiling waiter, who placed a plate with five fortune cookies in the center of the table.

"Me first!" Jessica said eagerly as she reached for one of the cookies.

The waiter looked from Elizabeth to Jessica and shook his head. "Two people who look exactly alike should share the same fortune, yes?" he asked.

"No! Just because we *look* alike," Elizabeth explained with a laugh, "doesn't mean we *act* alike!"

It was true that the twins did look like perfect copies of each other. Both girls had long blond hair streaked by the California sun, sparkling blue-green eyes, and tiny dimples in their left cheeks that appeared whenever they smiled.

But the similarities between them ended there. When it came to their personalities, it was very easy to tell the twins apart. Jessica was a member of the Unicorn Club, an exclusive group of the prettiest and most popular girls at Sweet Valley Middle School. She was fun-loving and spontaneous, and adored being the center of attention. She was also famous for cooking up outrageous schemes that often ended in disaster.

But when things went wrong, Jessica knew that she could always count on her sister for help. Elizabeth was more level-headed and reliable than her twin. She loved to read, and was very proud of her position as editor of the sixth-grade newspaper, *The Sweet Valley Sixers.* She and her friends were more interested in school than in cute boys or the latest fashions—two of the Unicorns' favorite topics.

In spite of their different personalities, however, Elizabeth and Jessica were the best of friends. Still, even loyal sisters like to tease each other now and then. And right then, Elizabeth couldn't help but laugh at Jessica's glum expression as she read her fortune.

"Come on, Jess," Elizabeth urged. "What does it say?"

Jessica frowned. "Nothing." She crumpled the strip of paper into a ball and tossed it across the table. "Who makes up these fortunes, anyway?"

Steven snatched the little piece of paper and began to unfold it.

"Steven!" Jessica cried. "My fortune is none of your business!"

"Jess, it's just for fun," Elizabeth pointed out. "You don't have to take it so seriously—"

"Listen to this!" Steven interrupted. "It's perfect!" He cleared his throat and Jessica glared furiously at him. "It says, 'Vanity is your greatest weakness'!"

The Wakefields laughed. Jessica *did* sometimes get preoccupied with her looks.

"I am *not* vain," Jessica muttered. "I just like to look my best, that's all."

While Steven continued to tease his sister, Elizabeth picked up her own fortune cookie. Slowly she pulled out the little strip of paper that was nestled inside. Avoid high places if you do not want to fall, she read silently.

As she gazed thoughtfully at the words, Elizabeth felt a strange chill run down the length of her spine.

"Come on, Elizabeth. Read it out loud," Jessica prompted. "It can't be any sillier than mine."

"It says, 'Avoid high places if you do not want to fall.' "

"Big deal." Jessica shrugged. "That's obvious. And you should stay out of the water if you don't want to get wet. At least your fortune wasn't insulting!" Suddenly Jessica's eyes lit up with inspiration. "Let's ask the waiter for some new cookies! I didn't like these fortunes at all."

"Well, my fortune says that I have to get home and catch up on the yard work," Mr. Wakefield said. "Tomorrow it's back to the office, and I still haven't trimmed those hedges."

"But we haven't done any shopping yet!" Jessica protested.

Mrs. Wakefield grinned. "We didn't come to the mall to shop. We came to have lunch. Besides, do you really want to start shopping again the day after Christmas?"

"Are you kidding?" Steven hooted. "Jessica wanted to go shopping the day after she was born!"

On the way home from the mall, Jessica and Elizabeth convinced Mr. Wakefield to drive past the harbor so that they could catch a glimpse of the carnival grounds. Several rides had already been assembled.

"Check out the roller coaster!" Steven exclaimed. He let out a low whistle.

"There's the Ferris wheel!" Jessica cried excitedly. She pointed toward the edge of the sandy beach, where workers were in the process of setting up the giant wheel. "I can't wait to ride it!" Jessica leaned toward the front seat. "I want to get there early tomorrow."

Mrs. Wakefield smiled. "Just promise me you aren't planning to have cotton candy for breakfast!"

"Don't worry," Jessica said lightly. "I won't be able to afford much cotton candy." She sighed dramatically. "My allowance just doesn't seem to last as long as it used to, and I spent all of the money I had saved on Christmas gifts."

Mr. and Mrs. Wakefield looked at each other.

"Wait a minute," Steven protested loudly. "If the munchkins get a bigger allowance, I should, too!"

"No one said anything about raising *anybody's* allowance," Mr. Wakefield cautioned. "But your mother and I will think it over."

Jessica grinned happily and turned to her sister. "What should we do first at the carnival, Elizabeth? Maybe we should start with the Ferris wheel. It's the biggest one I've ever seen! Look how high it's going to go!" Jessica exclaimed.

Elizabeth gazed thoughtfully at the huge wheel. "Yes," she agreed, "it's going to go very, very high."

"I am so bored!" Jessica moaned. She fell onto her bed and stared forlornly at the ceiling.

"Bored?" Elizabeth shook her head. "How can you possibly be bored? Mom and Dad just took us out to lunch. And Christmas was only yesterday!"

"But I don't have a single thing to do right *now*."

"You could try cleaning up your room," Elizabeth suggested with a grin. Jessica's bedroom always looked as if a tornado had just hit it.

"I *meant* that I want to do something fun. We have all this time off from school and I don't know what to do!"

"There's the carnival," Elizabeth offered.

"Not until tomorrow." Jessica pulled a pillow over her face. "Besides, I only have enough money for one day."

"I know something we could do today. And it wouldn't cost anything."

Jessica sat up excitedly. "What?"

"We could ride our bikes back down to the harbor and watch the carnival being set up."

"What a great idea! I was afraid you were going to suggest we spend the afternoon cleaning out my closet or something gross like that." Jessica jumped off her bed. "You know, Elizabeth, sometimes you actually *do* know how to have fun!"

The carnival was being set up on a wide field that ran alongside the beach, not far from the marina and only a ten-minute bike ride from the Wakefields' home.

"Look, Jessica," Elizabeth said as they reached the long gravel road that led to the carnival grounds. "The entrance is painted to look like a big clown's mouth."

The gravel made bike riding difficult, so the twins pulled off onto the grass and walked their bikes toward the brightly painted entrance. A small group of people were already gathered to watch the preparations.

"Elizabeth!" someone shouted. Elizabeth turned and saw Amy Sutton, her closest friend—after Jessica. Like Elizabeth, Amy wrote for *The Sweet Valley Sixers.*

Amy ran over to join the twins. She was carrying a spiral notebook and a pen.

"Hi, Amy. What's the notebook for?" Elizabeth asked.

"I thought I'd write a story about the carnival for the *Sixers.*"

"Great idea," Elizabeth said enthusiastically. "It can be the front-page story for our next issue."

"If you come across anything interesting," Amy said, "let me know."

Jessica rolled her eyes. "Winter break has just started and you two are already talking about school!"

"Jessica! Over here!"

Jessica glanced over her shoulder and spotted her friend Lila Fowler walking toward the carnival entrance with several other Unicorns. "I'm going to say hi to Lila."

"Meet me back here in half an hour, OK?" Elizabeth asked.

Jessica nodded and dashed off to join her friends.

"Hi, Jessica," Lila said as Jessica approached. "I tried to call and tell you we were coming down here, but there wasn't any answer."

"We went out to lunch at the mall," Jessica explained.

"Well, anyway, now that you're here, what do you think of my new sweater?" Lila asked. "It was a Christmas present from my father." Lila's father was one of the wealthiest men in Sweet Valley, and he spoiled Lila to make up for all the time he spent away on business trips.

Jessica hesitated. Lila's fuzzy pink sweater was covered with little tufts of white fur. Jessica thought that Lila looked a little bit like a rabbit.

"It's angora," Lila continued. "My father bought it when he was in England."

"We *know*, Lila," Belinda Layton said. "You've only mentioned it about fifty times in the past hour." Belinda, a sixth-grade Unicorn, had dark brown eyes and very short brown hair.

"Well, Jessica didn't know," Lila protested.

"It's very . . . uh, fuzzy," Jessica said at last.

Ellen Riteman, another sixth-grade Unicorn, spoke up. "Hey, let's walk along the fence and see what other rides there are."

"Let's head toward the beach," Jessica suggested. "That's where they're working on the Ferris wheel."

The girls followed the high chain-link fence that encircled the carnival until they came to the rides.

"Look! Bumper cars!" Ellen exclaimed. "I love those!"

"That's a kiddie ride," Lila declared. She pointed toward three workers who were attaching domed cars to a round platform. "Now, the Tilt-a-Whirl is a fun ride!"

"My little brother got sick on one of those once," Ellen remarked. "He went on it right after he'd eaten three corn dogs."

"Thanks for sharing that with us, Ellen," Belinda groaned.

The girls' attention was captured by two

workers, who were hammering a large sign into place over the entrance to a faded blue tent.

Lila read the gold lettering. "The Amazing Mademoiselle Z. The Future Revealed. Satisfaction Guaranteed."

"A fortune teller!" Jessica cried. "I was hoping the carnival would have one!"

"Give me a break!" Lila looked at Jessica skeptically. "You don't really believe this Mademoiselle Z person can tell the future, do you?"

"The sign says, SATISFACTION GUARANTEED," Jessica answered.

"Well, I think fortune tellers are all fakes." Lila began to move away, and the other Unicorns followed her. Jessica stayed behind for a moment, staring at Mademoiselle Z's intriguing sign. The Future Revealed, she read again.

I don't care what Lila says, Jessica vowed silently. *Tomorrow I'm going to pay a visit to Mademoiselle Z.*

"Can't you eat a little faster?" Jessica tapped her foot impatiently as Elizabeth swallowed her last spoonful of cereal.

"We have plenty of time, Jess," Elizabeth answered. "The carnival doesn't open for another twenty minutes. And it's just a ten-minute bike ride away."

"I know. But I want to be one of the first

people there. I've got it all planned out, Elizabeth. We'll start with the haunted house, then go on the roller coaster, then—"

"Wait a second!" Elizabeth interrupted, laughing. She took her cereal bowl to the sink and rinsed it out. "Let's do one thing at a time, OK?"

"OK." Jessica nodded solemnly. "But last one to the carnival has to set the table tonight. Ready, set, go!"

Before Elizabeth could protest, Jessica had dashed out the kitchen door. "Oh, no you don't, Jessica Wakefield!" Elizabeth muttered under her breath as she sprinted after her.

When the twins neared the carnival grounds, they paused for a moment on the grassy slope surrounding them to look at the large crowd that had already gathered at the carnival's entrance.

"What are we waiting for?" Jessica cried.

Once they had parked their bikes, the twins waited impatiently in line. When they finally reached the clown's-mouth entrance, they each bought a string of tickets.

"Each one of these tickets will admit you to one ride or game," the booth attendant explained. "Have fun!"

Jessica and Elizabeth were struck first by the long row of colorful food booths that stretched out before them. As they strolled along, they marveled at all the wonderful things to eat—caramel corn, saltwater taffy, candy apples, fudge, french fries, and corn dogs.

"Mmm! I smell cotton candy," Elizabeth said, taking a deep breath.

"Wait till Steven sees this!" Jessica laughed. "He won't know where to start!"

At the end of the row of food booths, the girls turned a corner and discovered a row of game booths. A long line of kids had already formed in front of the shooting gallery.

Suddenly Jessica stopped and pointed off to the left. "Look, there!" she said excitedly. "It's the haunted house!"

The twins raced toward a rickety-looking building on the edge of the carnival grounds. One window was covered over with boards and a sign over the door warned, ENTER IF YOU DARE. Elizabeth and Jessica gave their tickets to a man made up to look like Frankenstein's monster. His face was painted a sickly green, and a bolt was sticking out of either side of his neck. "Only two allowed in at a time," he growled. "Stay on the path, and have a *scary* trip!"

"He wasn't creepy at all," Jessica whispered as they walked through the door. "His makeup needs work."

The haunted house was pitch black and very cold. It made Elizabeth shiver. She could barely see Jessica standing beside her. Slowly, she began to take a step forward, and then hesitated. Normally she would never be frightened by something as childish as a haunted house, but for some reason Elizabeth had the strangest feeling that someone was watching her. She turned around to look, but in the dark she could see nothing. When she turned back, a skeleton dropped right in front of her.

Elizabeth screamed. She jumped back, bumped into something behind her, and screamed again.

"Give me a break, Elizabeth! It's just a plastic skeleton. You don't have to trample me!"

Jessica! Elizabeth had managed to forget all about her sister! She let out a sigh of relief.

Suddenly a door swung open ahead of them with a loud creak. Through the open door the twins could see a room lit with an eerie, bluish light that made Jessica's white shirt glow more brightly as they approached it.

The girls cautiously entered the room. Without any warning, a coffin sprang open and another skeleton shot out of it. Jessica jumped this time. "Give me a break, Jessica," Elizabeth mimicked her sister. "It's just a plastic skeleton!" Elizabeth felt better knowing that the haunted house made Jessica a little nervous, too.

The path led out of the second room and then turned sharply. As they rounded the turn, a witch dropped from the ceiling. She cackled loudly and her red eyes glowed brightly before she shot back up out of sight.

"She looked just like Mrs. Arnette does when I forget to do my social studies homework," Jessica joked. Mrs. Arnette was known for giving out tons of homework, and had been nicknamed "The Hairnet" because she always wore her hair in a bun.

A few steps further on, a huge ax blade came swinging down toward the twins and stopped just a few feet over their heads. Both girls were momentarily startled, and then began to giggle.

"You'd better watch what you say about Mrs. Arnette, Jessica!" Elizabeth told her twin.

"I always knew The Hairnet had eyes in the back of her head," Jessica answered, "but I didn't know she could hear me all the way across town!"

"Just be glad that Mrs. Arnette doesn't have an ax like that!" Elizabeth laughed. "Then you'd *definitely* have to do your homework!"

Just ahead, the path the girls were following split, and each fork led to a separate door. Over one door hung a sign that said VAMPIRES; over the other hung one marked GHOSTS.

The girls looked at each other questioningly. "Which one should we take?" Elizabeth asked.

"Let's each take a different one and then we can tell each other about it afterward," Jessica proposed. "I don't like ghosts, so I'll go through vampires."

"Do you really think we should split up?"

Jessica rolled her eyes. "Why not? Do you think the monsters will get us? I'll see you on the other side," she added in a spooky voice, "*if* you make it through alive!"

Elizabeth watched as her sister opened the door marked VAMPIRES and disappeared into a dark hallway. She glanced nervously over her shoulder. She was completely alone, but once again she felt as if she were being watched. Elizabeth started toward the door marked Ghosts, but when her hand touched the knob, she froze.

Suddenly, she had a terrible urge to run away.

Two

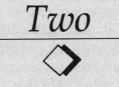

"Don't be afraid."

Elizabeth spun around to see who had spoken. It was a girl with solemn, dark eyes and long black hair. The girl was wearing an old-fashioned long white dress, and appeared to be a year or two younger than Elizabeth.

"Hello. My name is Claire," the girl said. "You don't have to be afraid. I've been through that room many times. My father owns this carnival."

Before Elizabeth could respond, the girl opened the door and stepped inside. Elizabeth followed right behind her, but when she got to the other side, the dark-haired girl had vanished. *She must have run ahead*, Elizabeth thought as she glanced around nervously.

A cold breeze blew through the room, and Elizabeth could feel the hair on the back of her neck stand up. *They must air-condition this room to give people the creeps,* she thought.

Ghostly figures hung in midair on both sides of the pathway, but the most frightening aspect of the room was the open grave ahead. Elizabeth realized that she would have to follow the path down into the grave. She gulped and walked toward the moss-covered tombstone. As she started down the steps that led into the grave, she noticed that carved into the stone were the initials *C.C.* and the dates *1882–1892*.

At the bottom of the grave, Elizabeth came to a door. She opened it cautiously. On the other side was a headless ghoul holding a sign that read, CONGRATULATIONS! YOU HAVE SURVIVED THE HAUNTED HOUSE. VISIT US AGAIN SOON!

Elizabeth continued toward a door marked Exit. Suddenly a shape leaped out from behind the ghoul.

Elizabeth shrieked as Jessica grabbed her around the neck. "Very funny, Jessica!" she said angrily. "You scared me half to death!"

Jessica laughed. "That was the idea." She looked at her twin questioningly. "So, how was the ghost room?"

"OK, I guess. You have to go through an open grave, which is a little gross."

Jessica nodded. "In the vampire room, you have to leave through an open casket. Same thing."

"Did you see that girl who went ahead of me?" Elizabeth asked.

"A girl?" Jessica repeated, widening her eyes. "No! She must have *disappeared into thin air!*"

"I'm serious, Jess." Elizabeth pushed open the exit door. "She said her parents own the carnival, and I thought I could get some information for the story Amy's writing."

"I didn't see anyone," Jessica said. "The vampire room and the ghost room both lead to the same place, and I was waiting for you behind that stupid zombie, or whatever it was. I would have seen anyone who came by."

"Well, she must have slipped past you." Elizabeth shielded her eyes from the bright sunshine and gazed across the crowd. "I think I see her now! I'm going to try and catch up with her. I'll see you later, Jessica."

Jessica tried to spot the dark-haired girl her sister had run after, but she could see no one. *Great!* she thought. *Now I'm stuck all by myself.* Jessica wondered if any of the Unicorns were around and set off to find her friends.

Jessica wandered around the carnival for a while, using almost all of her tickets on food and games. When she had only one ticket left and still had not come across any of the Unicorns, she decided to visit Mademoiselle Z.

Jessica made her way across the carnival grounds until she came to Mademoiselle Z's blue tent. A burly bald man, with a gold earring in one ear and a thick, jagged scar across his right cheek, stopped her at the entrance.

"Where do you think you're going?" he demanded gruffly.

"I—I wanted to have my fortune told," Jessica stammered.

"One ticket," the man muttered.

Jessica pulled the ticket from her pocket and handed it to the man. He smiled, revealing a shiny gold tooth. "You may enter," he told her as he stepped aside.

Jessica hesitated.

"Do not be afraid," said the bald man. "Mademoiselle Z will not harm you."

Jessica tried to smile as she stepped inside.

It was dark in the tent, almost as dark as the haunted house had been. Two candles flickered in a far corner, and a sweet aroma, like strong perfume, filled the air. On a table in the center of the tent sat a beautiful crystal ball, as big as a globe and perfectly clear. And behind the crystal ball sat Mademoiselle Z. Her long scarlet gown was covered with mirrored beads, and her shimmering black hair hung all the way to her waist.

"Sit down, my dear," she said. Her voice was almost a whisper.

Jessica sat in the elaborately carved wooden chair that faced Mademoiselle Z. "Is that a real crystal ball?" she asked reverently.

Mademoiselle Z nodded. "But of course." Her eyes were like a cat's—gold and glittery and full of mystery.

"And can you really tell the future?"

"You shall see for yourself." The fortune teller swept her palms over the glass globe. Her fingernails were very long and very red. "What is your name, my dear?" she asked in her soft, accented voice.

"Jessica." She sat up a little straighter in her chair. "Jessica Wakefield."

"And is there something special you'd like to ask when I consult my crystal ball?"

Jessica wondered. She hadn't really come prepared with any specific questions. For a moment she considered asking whether or not any of the boys at school had a crush on her, but decided that the question seemed a little personal for her first visit.

"Well?" the fortune teller prompted.

Jessica shook her head.

"Well, then," Mademoiselle Z said mysteriously, "we shall see what we shall see."

Jessica watched in fascination as the glamorous Mademoiselle Z closed her eyes and swirled her palms over the clear glass. She swayed back and forth in her chair as she chanted in a singsong voice:

> Ball of crystal,
> Eye of glass,
> Show me what
> Shall come to pass!

Suddenly, Mademoiselle Z sat very still. She opened her eyes and peered deep into the crystal ball. "Hmm," she said at last. "Very interesting, indeed."

"What?" Jessica asked eagerly.

"I see good things," Mademoiselle Z said softly. "Good things for Jessica Wakefield."

"You do?" Jessica leaned forward in her chair and squinted at the clear glass ball. "Why can't I see them, then?" she asked.

Mademoiselle Z shook her head patiently. "You cannot see because you do not have the gift, my child." She peered again into her crystal ball. "For you," she continued, "I see a happy event."

"When?" Jessica asked. "Can you tell me when?"

"Soon," she said with satisfaction. "Very soon." Mademoiselle Z closed her eyes and sighed heavily.

Jessica wasn't quite sure what she was supposed to do next. She waited for a moment, but Mademoiselle Z still didn't open her eyes. "Um . . . should I go now?"

"Yes. That is all," Mademoiselle Z answered softly.

At the door, Jessica paused to glance over her shoulder. Mademoiselle Z's eyes were still closed, and her hands rested lightly on the crystal ball.

As Jessica stepped back into the sunlight, she was once again startled by the sight of the huge bald man, still standing guard at the entrance to the tent. Jessica dashed away. Mademoiselle Z was definitely wonderful, but Jessica didn't care much for her assistant.

As she wandered back through the carnival grounds in search of Elizabeth, the fortune teller's words kept playing in her head over and over again. *A happy event . . . very soon!* She tried to imagine what it might be: a phone call from Bruce Patman, a trip to someplace exciting.

After a while, Jessica got tired of walking around and decided to start home without Elizabeth. She was just climbing onto her bike when she heard Elizabeth call her name.

"Jessica! Wait up!" Elizabeth ran toward the bike rack.

"Where have you been?" Jessica demanded. "I've been looking all over for you."

"Sorry. I was having so much fun that I guess I lost track of time."

As they rode home, Jessica told Elizabeth all about Mademoiselle Z and her wonderful prediction. "I can't wait for you to see her, Elizabeth," she finished. "She's the most amazing person I've ever met!"

"I met someone really interesting, too," Elizabeth said. "Claire—the girl who passed me in the haunted house. She's a couple of years younger than we are, but she acts so grown-up."

"Don't you think you should hang around with people your own age?" Jessica asked bluntly.

"Claire's different. She seems older, probably because she's traveled so much. Remember, I told you her parents own the carnival," Elizabeth replied.

When the twins arrived home, they found Mrs. Wakefield in the living room. "How was the carnival, girls?" she asked, putting aside the newspaper she had been reading.

"Great," Jessica said as she settled beside her mother on the couch.

"Please tell me that you didn't eat mountains of junk food. We're having spaghetti and meatballs tonight, and I'd hate to think you'd ruined your appetites," Mrs. Wakefield said.

"My favorite dinner!" Jessica exclaimed. "I always have room for that."

Mrs. Wakefield smiled. "I've also got some good news for you two. Your father and I have been giving it some thought, and we feel that you've both earned a raise in your allowances for the new year."

Jessica's jaw dropped open in amazement. Suddenly Mademoiselle Z's words came back to her. *Something good will happen . . . soon.* Her prediction had come true!

"That's wonderful, Mom!" Elizabeth gave her mother a hug.

"Hey, what about me?" Steven came into the living room, carrying a basketball in one hand and a sandwich in the other. "Don't I deserve a raise?" he asked hopefully. "After all, everyone knows I do all the chores around here."

"Everyone knows you do all the *eating* around here, you mean," Jessica remarked.

"Of course you're included, Steven," Mrs. Wakefield answered.

"All right!" he exclaimed, tossing his basketball into the air.

"See, Elizabeth?" Jessica said excitedly. "Mademoiselle Z was right! She really *can* tell the future!"

"Mademoiselle Z?" Mrs. Wakefield repeated.

"Jessica went to a fortune teller at the carnival," Elizabeth explained.

"Wait until the Unicorns hear about this," Jessica continued. "Mom, do you think I could go back to the carnival tonight? It's open late."

"I suppose I could drive you over after dinner," Mrs. Wakefield decided. "But just tonight. Let's not make a habit of it, OK?"

"You're the greatest!" Jessica cried as she rushed toward the stairway.

"Wait a minute, Jess," Elizabeth called. "Where are you going? It's time to set the table."

"I'm going to call Lila and the rest of the Unicorns to tell them about Mademoiselle Z," Jessica explained breathlessly. "Tonight they can see her amazing powers for themselves!"

After dinner, Mrs. Wakefield drove the twins and several of the Unicorns back to the carnival. Elizabeth went off on her own to spend time with her new friend, Claire, which was just fine with Jessica. Personally, she couldn't see the point of hanging around with someone so much younger— even if her parents *did* own the whole carnival.

"Can we go see Mademoiselle Z now?" Jessica asked Lila impatiently as they stood at the dart-throw booth. After eight tries, Lila had finally won a T-shirt with a picture of Johnny Buck, the Unicorns' favorite rock star, on the front.

Lila handed Jessica the chocolate milk shake she had been drinking and put the T-shirt on over her blouse. "Isn't it a great shirt?" she asked, parading in front of the other Unicorns. "I just knew I would win."

"After eight tries, who wouldn't?" Jessica muttered under her breath as she led the way to Mademoiselle Z.

"Who is that creepy guy?" Ellen murmured as they approached the tent. She pointed to the burly bald man with the gold earring, who was still standing guard.

"Don't worry," Jessica answered a little nervously. "Just give him your ticket and go straight inside."

As the Unicorns crowded into the small tent, Mademoiselle Z looked up from her crystal ball and smiled serenely at Jessica. "Ah, Jessica Wakefield," she said in her soft, wispy voice. "I see you have brought some friends."

"You were right about the good thing happening," Jessica told her. "It was like a miracle!"

"A raise in your allowance is hardly a miracle, Jessica," Lila whispered sarcastically.

"Your friend has doubts." Mademoiselle Z looked darkly at Lila.

"You can see right through that glass ball," Lila muttered to Ellen. "Fortune tellers are fakes, you know."

"Enough!" Mademoiselle Z shouted. She glared directly at Lila, and her eyes glowed like hot coals. "Mark my words!" she hissed. "Before this night is over, you will see great misfortune!"

Jessica's eyes widened, but Lila just shrugged indifferently. Some of the other Unicorns even snickered.

"Come on, you guys," Lila said. "What a waste of a good ticket!" She took a drink of her milk shake and led the group out the door.

Only Jessica lagged behind. "I'm sorry," she said softly.

Mademoiselle Z smiled. "Come and see me again."

Jessica left the tent and ran to catch up with the Unicorns. She found them watching a small spotted horse being led by a worker in overalls.

Lila stepped forward to pet the horse, but as she did, the horse suddenly reared up and flailed at the air with its hooves. Lila jumped back, tripped over a rope that supported a nearby tent, and landed in a mud puddle. Her new Johnny Buck T-shirt was covered with the remains of her chocolate milk shake.

For a moment no one moved. At last Ellen reached down and extended her hand to Lila.

"My new T-shirt," Lila moaned as Ellen helped pull her out of the puddle. "It's ruined!" Lila tried to wipe some of the milk shake off the shirt, but her muddied hands only made it dirtier than before.

"It looks to me as if Mademoiselle Z's not such a fake after all, Lila," Belinda remarked.

Something made Jessica turn from watching Lila try to clean herself off, and as she did she spotted Elizabeth only a few feet away. Jessica called to her, but Elizabeth walked right on by, as though she hadn't heard or seen a thing.

Three

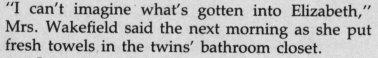

"I can't imagine what's gotten into Elizabeth," Mrs. Wakefield said the next morning as she put fresh towels in the twins' bathroom closet.

Jessica stopped drying her hair and turned to face her mother. "What do you mean, Mom?"

"She was in such a hurry to get to the carnival this morning that she didn't even make her bed."

"I wondered where she was," Jessica said. "Why didn't she wait for me so we could go together?"

Mrs. Wakefield shook her head. "I don't know, honey. When I went downstairs to make coffee this morning, there was a note from Elizabeth on the kitchen table. It said she planned to be at the carnival all day."

Jessica glanced into Elizabeth's room through

the open bathroom door. Elizabeth's bed was unmade, and a small pile of clothes lay on the floor.

"And while we're on the subject of unmade beds," Mrs. Wakefield said, "*your* room could use its once-a-year cleanup."

"You mean *before* I go to the carnival?" Jessica groaned.

"That was the general idea, yes," Mrs. Wakefield said dryly.

"OK, Mom." Jessica glanced at her twin's room again, remembering all the times Elizabeth had helped out when she had forgotten to do her chores. "I suppose I could make Elizabeth's bed, too," she added reluctantly.

"Thanks, Jessica," Mrs. Wakefield said with obvious surprise. "I'm sure your sister will appreciate it."

Just then the phone rang. "I'll get it!" Jessica ran to the telephone in the hallway and picked up the receiver.

"You're not going to the carnival today, are you?" Lila demanded as soon as Jessica had said hello.

"Sure I am," Jessica responded. "Aren't you?"

"After I was nearly killed by that wild horse?"

"It was a pony," Jessica pointed out. "Don't you think you're exaggerating a little?"

"No," Lila said defensively. "I don't want to

have anything to do with Mademoiselle Z and that stupid carnival."

Jessica couldn't wait to see the fortune teller again, but she could tell there was no point in arguing with Lila.

"Anyway, I have something much more exciting to tell you," Lila continued. "My dad's going to let me have a New Year's Eve party! I can invite as many people as I want, and he's even going to hire a live band!"

"That's great!" Jessica exclaimed. Lila's parties were always fun.

"Will you help me plan it?" Lila asked. "We only have a few days till New Year's Eve."

"Sure. Maybe we could come up with a theme and make special decorations," Jessica added.

"That's a wonderful idea!" Lila said. "Why don't you come over to my house? I've already started a list of people I want to invite."

Jessica hesitated. "I would, but—"

"But you'd rather go to the carnival, right?" Lila interrupted.

"We could plan the party tomorrow," Jessica suggested.

"Fine," Lila snapped. "But if I were you, I'd stay away from that stupid fortune teller!"

"Actually," Jessica said, "the *first* thing I'm going to do when I get there is to visit Mademoiselle Z. Want me to ask her how your party's going to turn out?"

"I don't need a fortune teller to tell me that!" Lila scoffed. "I'll talk to you later, Jessica—unless, of course, you're trampled to death by wild horses."

As she hung up the phone, Jessica couldn't help smiling. How could Lila be so wrong about Mademoiselle Z?

Jessica headed to her bedroom to get dressed. After several minutes of staring into her closet, she felt completely frustrated. "I don't have a single thing to wear!"

Jessica decided to borrow the new yellow blouse Elizabeth had received for Christmas. But when she checked Elizabeth's closet, the blouse was gone. Apparently Elizabeth had decided to wear it that morning.

Jessica tramped back to her own closet and decided to wear a yellow T-shirt of her own with her jeans. As she examined her reflection in the mirror, she hesitated for a moment. With Elizabeth probably wearing jeans with her yellow blouse, it might seem as if the twins were deliberately trying to dress alike. When they were younger, the girls had always worn identical outfits. But when they'd started middle school, they were careful to dress differently.

Still, Jessica decided, a blouse and a T-shirt

weren't *exactly* alike. And she'd already wasted enough time trying to decide what to wear!

Jessica spent the next few minutes cleaning up as quickly as she could. As she ran downstairs to have breakfast, she heard a knock at the front door. She swung open the door to find Amy Sutton waiting on the front porch. Her blue ten-speed bicycle was parked in the driveway.

"Hi, Jessica," Amy said. "Where's Elizabeth?"

"At the carnival. She left early this morning," Jessica replied.

"The carnival?" Amy repeated in surprise. "But we were supposed to go bike riding and work on our article this morning."

Jessica shrugged. "I guess she forgot."

"That's strange," Amy muttered. "She doesn't usually forget things like this."

"Well, she *does* have a new friend, Amy," Jessica explained bluntly. She knew Amy would feel a little jealous of Claire.

Amy frowned. "A new friend?"

"A girl named Claire. Her parents own the carnival." Jessica looked at Amy's unhappy face and felt a twinge of guilt. "Personally, I don't know why she likes this girl so much," she added. "She's a lot younger. I can't imagine what they have in common! Anyway, I'm sure Elizabeth will call you when she gets home."

"I wanted to tell her about some research I

did at the library yesterday afternoon." Amy said. "There seems to be something odd about the Caldwell Carnival."

"The Caldwell Carnival?" Jessica asked.

"Yes, that's what it's called. I found some articles about it in old newspapers," Amy explained. "The carnival was forced to leave two other towns in the state before the end of its scheduled run. In one of the towns, a girl fell off a ride and was injured. And there were rumors of other strange things happening to kids who visited the carnival."

Jessica remembered what had happened to Lila the night before. "What kind of strange things?"

"I don't exactly know." Amy pushed a strand of hair out of her eyes. "The stories were pretty vague. That's why I was hoping Elizabeth could help me do some more research today."

"I guess she's doing her own research," Jessica said. "*At* the carnival. If I see her there, I'll tell her you stopped by."

"Thanks, Jessica," Amy said. "And while you're there, keep your eyes open, OK?"

"For what?" Jessica wanted to know.

"I don't know." Amy frowned. "Anything strange, I guess."

Elizabeth stopped near the noisy shooting gallery to search the crowd for Claire. She'd looked all over the carnival grounds for her new friend, but so far she had seen no sign of her. "Maybe I'd better ask someone where she is," Elizabeth murmured.

"I'm right here, Elizabeth," a voice said.

Elizabeth spun around to find Claire standing a few feet away. For a moment, Elizabeth was puzzled. How had Claire heard her over the noise of the shooting gallery?

"You get used to the noise, Elizabeth," Claire said, as if she had guessed what Elizabeth was thinking.

Elizabeth shook her head. "You're amazing, Claire."

"I *am?*" Claire laughed with delight.

"It was as if you'd just read my mind!" Elizabeth said.

"That's because we're so much alike, Elizabeth," Claire said happily. She reached for Elizabeth's hand. "Let's go for a walk."

As Claire led the way through the thick crowd, Elizabeth couldn't help but watch her curiously. She'd never met anyone quite like Claire. There was an old-fashioned quality about her that fascinated Elizabeth. In part it was Claire's look— her ivory skin and her huge brown eyes with their thick fringe of lashes. And Claire dressed oddly, too. Both of the times Elizabeth had seen her, Claire had been wearing an old-fashioned white dress with a round lace collar and a big starched bow in back.

"My mom has a picture of her great-grandmother when she was a little girl, and she's wearing a dress that looks just like yours," Elizabeth told Claire as they paused to watch the bumper cars. "That dress you have on must be very old."

"No, it's new, Elizabeth," Claire answered.

Elizabeth frowned. Where would Claire have found such an old-fashioned style? "Where did you buy it?" she asked.

Claire gazed at two little boys who were trying to smash their bumper cars into each other. "This is my second-favorite dress," she said, smiling. "My very favorite dress got torn." She paused for a moment, and her smile faded. "It was blue and cream—my two favorite colors in the whole world."

"Those are my favorite colors, too!" Elizabeth exclaimed. "In fact, my bedroom is blue and cream."

Claire turned to Elizabeth. Her brown eyes shone so beautifully that Elizabeth couldn't help but stare into them. "You see, Elizabeth?" Claire said. "I *told* you we were a lot alike!"

The girls strolled past the rows of food booths. "I'm very glad you came to play with me today, Elizabeth," Claire said. "I don't have any friends to play with."

"Aren't there any other kids who travel with the carnival?"

"No." Claire shook her head solemnly. "I'm all alone."

It seemed strange to Elizabeth that a person could be unhappy living with a carnival full of things to do. After all, Claire must have made friends with some of the men and women who worked there.

"The people who work here don't like me," Claire said bluntly.

Again, Elizabeth had the odd feeling that Claire was reading her thoughts. "They don't?" Elizabeth asked.

"No. Because I'm the owner's daughter, they all think I spy for my father." Claire tossed her hair back over her shoulders. "They ignore me and pretend I'm not here. You'll see."

"But why would they ignore you?" Elizabeth pressed. Claire seemed like such a friendly girl. "Have you tried to be friendly with them?"

"They will never be my friends," Claire stated crisply. She turned to Elizabeth and smiled broadly. "Besides, now I have you, Elizabeth."

Elizabeth hated to think of Claire being so lonely. "Don't you have any brothers or sisters?" she asked.

Claire shook her head. "No. No brothers or sisters."

"I have a sister," Elizabeth said. "Her name is Jessica and we're—" Suddenly she stopped in mid-sentence. Claire had completely disappeared!

"Claire?" Elizabeth called. She spun around, scanning the crowd for any sign of her friend. "This is ridiculous!" Elizabeth muttered under her breath. How could a person just vanish into thin air?

"Here's a sno-cone for you, Elizabeth."

"Claire!" Elizabeth gasped. "Where did you go?"

"I went to get you this. It's root beer." Claire handed Elizabeth a paper cone filled with brown ice.

"But how did you know I wanted one?" Elizabeth sputtered.

"Root beer's my favorite flavor," Claire said.

"Mine, too!" Elizabeth said. "But you still haven't answered my question, Claire!"

Claire smiled. Her brown eyes glowed warmly. "Would you like to see a trick?"

Elizabeth laughed. "I think I just did!"

"Try thinking of a number," Claire instructed.

"All right," Elizabeth agreed. She thought of the number twelve, her age.

"No, I mean a *big* number. Not something so easy!" Claire said. She crossed her arms over her chest impatiently.

"But I haven't even told you what it is!" Elizabeth protested.

Claire smiled patiently. "A very large number, Elizabeth."

Elizabeth closed her eyes.

"Two thousand five hundred and seventy-eight," Claire said.

Elizabeth's eyes flew open and she nearly dropped her sno-cone. "How did you do that?" she demanded. There was no logical way Claire could have guessed correctly—but she had!

"I'll teach you," Claire said. "When you are ready."

Elizabeth shook her head disbelievingly. "Hold this, will you?" Elizabeth asked. She handed the sno-cone to Claire, reached into her backpack and pulled out a small notebook and a pen.

"What are you doing, Elizabeth?" Claire asked.

"I'm taking notes. My friend and I are going to write an article about the carnival for *The Sweet Valley Sixers*, our class newspaper," Elizabeth explained. "And the first thing I want to know is how you just managed to do that trick!"

"You'll find out soon," Claire said with a laugh. "I'll tell you all about the carnival. And I'll show you secret places no one else can go."

"This is going to be a great article!" Elizabeth exclaimed. "Thanks to you, Claire." She looked at Claire quizzically. "I still say it should have been impossible for you to guess that number correctly," Elizabeth said.

"Nothing is impossible, Elizabeth," Claire said simply. "Come on. I'll take you to see the ponies now. I love horses."

"So do I," Elizabeth said. By now it no longer surprised her that she and Claire shared the same interests. "A friend of mine owns a horse named Thunder, and I get to ride him whenever I want to. In fact, I'd like to own a horse someday. Of course, I'd have to live in a house with lots of land around it."

"Or you could live in a carnival," Claire suggested. "You could come live with me."

Elizabeth laughed, but there was something in Claire's eyes that made Elizabeth think her friend might almost be serious.

Claire led Elizabeth to the stable where the ponies for the pony ride were kept. "You can go in and pet them," Claire said. "Most of the ponies are being ridden, but there are always a couple of extra ones in the stable."

"Aren't you coming in, too?" Elizabeth asked.

"The ponies are afraid of me," Claire said sadly. "I'd like to pet them and feed them, but they don't get along with me very well."

Claire opened the stable door. Inside there were two ponies, each in its own stall. "The brown one is named Jasper, and the black and white one is called Old Spots. Go on. You can pet them."

"We could do something else," Elizabeth offered.

"No. They like to be petted. They just don't like *me*," Claire explained.

Elizabeth wondered if Claire was secretly afraid of the ponies. Maybe she just didn't want to admit it to Elizabeth.

Elizabeth stepped into the stable and inhaled the sweet smell of fresh hay. She approached Old Spots and stroked his head. "Hi, boy," she whispered. "You're a pretty one, aren't you? I'm sorry I don't have any sugar to give you. Next time I come, I'll bring you something good to eat."

Elizabeth moved on to Jasper, who had a long, beautiful mane and deep brown eyes. Elizabeth ran her fingers through his mane and the horse nuzzled her ear.

Elizabeth heard a sound behind her and turned to see Claire approaching. Jasper let out a loud whinny.

Claire stepped closer and Jasper reared up on his hind legs. Elizabeth spun around to see his hooves flashing like daggers in the air behind her head. She screamed and dropped to the floor.

Jasper's hooves flew so close to Elizabeth's head that she could feel the breeze they made.

The horse whinnied again and backed all the way into his stall.

"Are you all right, Elizabeth?" Claire asked.

"Yes, but I almost *wasn't* all right!" Elizabeth answered in a shaky voice.

"I shouldn't have come into the stable, but I thought that maybe this time . . ." Claire's voice trailed off. "I told you they didn't like me."

"Why *did* you come in, if you knew they were going to react that way?" Elizabeth asked. "I could have been hurt, Claire!"

"I'm really sorry, Elizabeth," Claire said in a small voice.

"That's OK," Elizabeth said quickly. "I'm fine now."

As soon as they were back outside in the bright sunlight, Elizabeth felt better. Still, several minutes passed before her knees stopped shaking.

The girls decided to rest on a grassy area near the edge of the carnival grounds. The area was deserted, except for a small blue tent off to one side and partially hidden behind a row of food booths.

"I've never seen horses react that way for no reason," Elizabeth said. "I wonder why they don't like you?"

"I don't *know*, " Claire said unhappily. "They just don't!" Her eyes filled with tears and her lower lip began to tremble.

"It's all right, Claire," Elizabeth said sympathetically. "It's not worth crying over."

"You're so nice, Elizabeth," Claire said, brightening quickly. "Will you come and see me every day?"

"*Every* day? Well, I guess I could stop by for a little while each day, for as long as the carnival is in town. Of course, then I'll have to go back to school."

"Every day!" Claire jumped to her feet. "That's wonderful!"

"There's just one condition," Elizabeth said as she stood up. "You've got to promise to explain to me how you do those mind-reading tricks."

"I promise," Claire said happily.

Elizabeth gazed off at the crowds of people before them, wondering if Jessica had arrived yet with the Unicorns. Then she noticed a movement at the door to the small blue tent.

A woman stepped out and looked up at the sun. She wore a beautiful red dress with mirrored beads that sparkled as she moved. As the woman turned her gaze toward Elizabeth and Claire, her face suddenly darkened.

"Who is that woman?" Elizabeth asked.

"No one important," Claire said. "Just a crazy old woman. I wish my father had gotten rid of her a long time ago."

Four

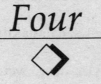

Jessica rode her bike up to the carnival entrance and hopped off. "Well," she said under her breath, "I see Elizabeth is still here." Elizabeth's bike was carefully locked to the bike rack.

Jessica gazed around her excitedly. Beyond the carnival grounds the sea was calm and partly hidden by morning fog, but the sun was shining brightly overhead.

As soon as she had purchased some tickets, Jessica began to look for her sister. But the carnival was very crowded, and after almost half an hour Jessica still hadn't found her.

At last Jessica decided to go back to Mademoiselle Z's tent without Elizabeth. The man with the scar was not at his usual post outside the tent, and for a minute Jessica wondered if Mademoiselle Z was gone as well. But when Jessica peeked inside, she saw Mademoiselle Z sitting calmly in front of her crystal ball. Her eyes were closed, and Jessica had to cough to get her attention.

Mademoiselle Z's eyes opened slowly. "You!" she cried suddenly, pointing at Jessica with one long finger.

"Y-yes," Jessica said shakily. "It's me, Jessica Wakefield, and I—"

"I know who you are," Mademoiselle Z interrupted, lowering her voice. "And I know your friend, too."

"Lila?" Jessica asked.

"Is *that* what she calls herself?" Mademoiselle Z grimaced.

"I—I just wanted my future told again," Jessica said nervously.

"Sit then." Mademoiselle Z pointed to the chair and Jessica sat down obediently. The fortune teller looked deep into her crystal ball as she rocked back and forth. "You want to know your future, Jessica Wakefield? I will tell you your future."

Jessica leaned forward, transfixed by Mademoiselle Z's glittering eyes.

"You will have no future, Jessica Wakefield," she pronounced abruptly.

Jessica gulped. "What do you mean?"

"I mean what I said. *You will have no future— unless you stay away from this carnival!*"

Jessica's heart seemed to jump into her throat. She leaped to her feet so suddenly that her knee slammed into Mademoiselle Z's table. Jessica watched in horror as the crystal ball wobbled on its stand. She tried desperately to catch it, but the ball toppled from the table and rolled across the floor.

"Out! Out!" Mademoiselle Z shouted. "Out of my tent! And if you value your life, you will never return to this carnival!"

Jessica fled. She didn't stop running until she had left the carnival grounds and was halfway across the surrounding grassy field. Only then did she realize that she had left her bike behind.

"Now what?" she cried out loud. "I'm cursed. I'm cursed, and I don't even have my bike!"

Jessica was too scared to go back by herself. "Where is Elizabeth when I really need her?" she moaned. Then she decided it was probably safe to go back for her bicycle as long as she didn't go beyond the clown's-mouth entrance to the actual carnival grounds.

As she headed back toward the carnival entrance, she spotted Elizabeth in the crowd. "Lizzie!" she shouted, but Elizabeth didn't seem to hear her. "Elizabeth!" Jessica screamed as loudly as she could.

Elizabeth continued to walk along slowly. At

the exit, she turned and waved to someone whom Jessica could not see.

Elizabeth exited through the big clown's-mouth gate, and suddenly noticed Jessica. "Hi, Jess!" she called.

"It's about time!" Jessica cried. "Let's get our bikes and get out of here!"

"Did you see Claire?" Elizabeth asked. "The dark-haired girl I was with?"

"Who?" Jessica demanded.

"Claire," Elizabeth repeated. "She just walked me to the gate."

"I didn't see anyone, Elizabeth," Jessica snapped. "And anyway, who cares about your silly friends? *I've been cursed!*"

"I am never, *ever* going back to that carnival again!" Jessica exclaimed when the twins arrived home. "Never!"

"Don't you think you're overreacting, Jessica?" Elizabeth asked as she led the way to the kitchen. "I can't believe you're taking all this fortune-telling stuff so seriously."

"But I told you what happened to Lila!" Jessica said. She picked up the cookie jar and carried it to the kitchen table. "Mademoiselle Z has amazing powers, Elizabeth!"

"What's the Z stand for?" Steven asked as he entered the kitchen. "Zany?"

Jessica took an oatmeal cookie from the jar and ignored her brother's remark. "You should have seen her face when I knocked over her crystal ball, Elizabeth. I was scared to death!" She lowered her voice. "Personally, I don't think you should go back to the carnival, either."

"But I have to go back!" Elizabeth insisted.

"Why?" Jessica wanted to know. "You've seen all the attractions already."

"I promised Claire," Elizabeth said. "And I want to do some more research for the *Sixers* article. Besides," she added, smiling, "I don't believe in curses."

"Curses?" Steven repeated, raising an eyebrow. He grabbed a handful of cookies and sat down. "Who got cursed?"

"Jessica thinks the fortune teller at the carnival put a curse on her," Elizabeth explained.

"I *know* she put a curse on me!" Jessica said defensively. "She said that unless I stayed away from the carnival, I wouldn't have a future."

"Awesome!" Steven said. "I wonder if I could get her to put a curse on a whole basketball team?"

"Steven!" Jessica cried. "This is *serious!*"

"I *am* serious." Steven chewed thoughtfully on a cookie. "We've got a tough basketball game against Westover High next week. They're undefeated this season, and we can use all the help we can get! Where can I find this Z lady, anyway?"

"My life is in danger, and all you can think about is basketball!" Jessica said indignantly.

"Jessica," Elizabeth said calmly, "I really think you need to be more logical about this. Mademoiselle Z can't see into the future, and she certainly can't put curses on people!"

"But just in case she really can," Steven said with a sly smile, "can I have your stereo, Jessica?"

Jessica crossed her arms over her chest. "Just wait until someone puts a curse on you, Steven Wakefield! See how sympathetic I'll be then."

Steven took another handful of cookies. "I already *am* cursed," he responded. "With twin sisters!" He dashed from the kitchen before either girl could respond.

Jessica sighed dramatically. "Anyway," she continued, "I still don't see why you want to go back to the carnival, now that you know about Mademoiselle Z's curse."

"I want to spend more time with Claire," Elizabeth explained. She went to the refrigerator to get some milk. "After all, the carnival won't be in town that much longer. And she seems so lonely."

Jessica narrowed her eyes. "Why is she so lonely? Doesn't she have any friends?"

Elizabeth took a drink of her milk. "There aren't any other kids Claire's age traveling with the carnival. And the workers don't like her because her parents own the carnival."

"Maybe they don't like her because she's just not very likable," Jessica suggested. "What else do you know about Claire?" she asked. "Have you met her family?"

"No," Elizabeth said.

"Where does she stay while the carnival's in town? In one of those big trailers we saw near the edge of the grounds?" Jessica asked.

Elizabeth shrugged. "I don't know. She's never mentioned it."

"You've spent all this time with her, and you don't know anything about her?" Jessica demanded.

"I know that I like her," Elizabeth replied. "There's something unique about Claire—something old-fashioned."

"Sounds boring," Jessica said.

"She's not, Jess. She can do these amazing mind-reading tricks. She said she'd teach me how to do them. I know you'd like her if you met her. Maybe you could spend the day with us tomorrow," Elizabeth suggested.

"At the carnival?" Jessica rolled her eyes. "No way! Besides, I have my own friends."

Suddenly Jessica remembered Amy's visit to the house that morning. Maybe a little dose of guilt would cure Elizabeth of her fascination with Claire. "By the way," Jessica said casually, "Amy stopped by this morning. She said you had made plans to go bike riding and work on the *Sixers* article with her."

"Oh, no!" Elizabeth's hand flew to her mouth. "I completely forgot about Amy this morning! Was she upset?"

Jessica nodded solemnly. "I think her feelings were really hurt."

"I feel terrible!" Elizabeth moaned. "I'll have to think of a way to make it up to her."

"Anyway, Amy seems to think there's something weird about the carnival," Jessica remarked.

"What do you mean?" Elizabeth asked.

"I don't know exactly." Jessica shrugged. "Something about it getting kicked out of a few towns recently."

"Hmm," Elizabeth murmured. "I'll have to ask her what she found out."

"By the way, Elizabeth," Jessica added, "meeting Amy wasn't the only thing you forgot about this morning. You owe your eternal gratitude to a certain very thoughtful person who just happens to be your twin."

"I do?" Elizabeth said doubtfully. "Why?"

"Go look at your room and you'll see," Jessica answered.

"Oh, no. I forgot to make my bed, didn't I?" Elizabeth guessed.

Jessica nodded. "Very un-Lizzielike."

Elizabeth followed Jessica upstairs. "I was in

such a hurry to get to the carnival this morning, I completely forgot to clean up my room."

When they reached the door to Elizabeth's bedroom, Jessica pointed out how neatly she had made the bed.

"Thanks, Jess," Elizabeth said gratefully.

"That's OK. After all, you're always covering for me. It was fun to reverse roles and help *you* for a change!" Jessica remarked.

"Well, I hope I won't need your services again any time soon," Elizabeth said sheepishly.

"Me, too!" Jessica said with a laugh. "It's hard enough making my own bed. I don't want to have to do yours again, especially not after the major cleaning I did today. Come see my room. You won't even recognize it!"

Elizabeth stood at the doorway to her twin's room. "Jessica!" she exclaimed. "I didn't realize you had pink carpeting in here! It's always been covered with a layer of dirty clothes!"

"Very funny, Elizabeth," Jessica responded. "I even straightened up my fashion magazines, see?"

As she turned to point out the neat stack of magazines, Jessica caught sight of a strange figure outside the window. "Who's that?" she muttered, moving closer for a better look.

A man in a black hat and a long black raincoat stood across the street. He was staring directly at her bedroom window. Jessica had an uneasy sense of recognition, but she couldn't quite place him. Then the man turned and walked away slowly.

"Jessica?" Elizabeth asked from the doorway. "Who was it?"

"I don't know. Probably no one," Jessica said, trying to ignore the goose bumps rising on her skin. Quickly she pulled down her window shade. "Let's go have some more cookies, Elizabeth," she said brightly. "But promise me one thing."

"What?" Elizabeth wanted to know.

"No more talk about the carnival!" Jessica declared.

Five

◇

The next morning, Elizabeth woke up before her alarm clock was set to go off. She leaped out of bed and dressed as quickly as she could.

Mrs. Wakefield was in the kitchen making coffee when Elizabeth came downstairs to have breakfast. "What got you up so bright and early?" Mrs. Wakefield asked with a smile.

"I'm going to the carnival," Elizabeth said eagerly.

"Again?" Mrs. Wakefield shook her head. "Isn't it getting a bit boring?"

Elizabeth poured herself a glass of orange juice. "I've met a girl named Claire there. Her parents own the carnival," she explained. "We've become good friends."

"Speaking of friends," Mrs. Wakefield said,

"did Jessica tell you that Amy stopped by yesterday to see you?"

"Amy!" Elizabeth exclaimed. "I nearly forgot again!"

She ran to the telephone and picked up the receiver. But as she started to dial Amy's number, Elizabeth pictured lonely, dark-eyed Claire standing before her. She had no choice. She had to get back to the carnival. Elizabeth replaced the receiver, vowing to herself that she would call Amy just as soon as she got back that afternoon.

"Why didn't you call Amy, honey?" Mrs. Wakefield asked.

Elizabeth shrugged. "I was afraid it was too early."

"Well, try to get in touch with her today," Mrs. Wakefield said. "You wouldn't want to hurt her feelings just because you have a new friend."

"I will," Elizabeth promised.

"And be sure you're home by five-thirty," Mrs. Wakefield added. "We haven't really seen much of you lately."

"I promise, Mom." Elizabeth walked over and gave her mother a hug.

"One more bit of motherly advice, OK?" Mrs. Wakefield said with a grin.

"Sure." Elizabeth smiled. "What?"

Mrs. Wakefield pointed to Elizabeth's feet. "Did you get dressed in the dark?"

Elizabeth looked down and groaned. She'd been in such a hurry to get dressed that she'd put on one blue sock and one red one!

As Elizabeth parked her bike at the carnival, her eyes were drawn to the ocean. Wisps of early morning fog still hovered over the water.

"Elizabeth!" a voice called.

Elizabeth spun around to see Julie Porter waving. Julie was a good friend who worked on *The Sweet Valley Sixers* with Amy and Elizabeth.

"Hi, Julie," Elizabeth called back. She waited as her friend ran over to join her.

"I'm going to the carnival," Julie said. "Have you been here already?"

Elizabeth nodded. "Lots of times. It's really great."

"Have you been on all the rides?" Julie asked as they walked toward the entrance.

"Well, no," Elizabeth admitted. "Actually, I've made friends with the daughter of the carnival owners. She takes me to all sorts of places where visitors aren't usually allowed."

"Do you think she would take me, too?" Julie asked excitedly.

"That's a great idea!" Elizabeth said. "I'm sure Claire would like to meet you. We could all spend the day together!"

The girls walked through the clown's-mouth

entrance. "Where do we go to find your friend?" Julie asked.

"She's usually just hanging around some- where. She'll turn up," Elizabeth said.

"Wow!" Julie exclaimed, gazing at all the brightly painted booths and whizzing rides. "I should have come here sooner! I'll bet there are a million fun things to—" Suddenly she fell silent.

Elizabeth looked anxiously at her friend. Julie's face had grown very pale, and her eyes looked wild with fear.

"I have to go home!" Julie said frantically.

"What?" Elizabeth asked in amazement. "I thought—"

"I have to go home *right now!*" Julie insisted.

"But why?" Elizabeth wanted to know.

"I . . . I don't know. I just have to or—" Julie hesitated, shaking her head in confusion. "I have to go, Elizabeth!" she cried. Without another word, she turned and ran toward the exit.

Elizabeth began to follow Julie. She'd only gone a few steps when she heard a familiar voice behind her.

"Hello, Elizabeth."

"Claire!" Elizabeth exclaimed. "That was my friend Julie, and she just ran out of here like—like she was scared half to death!"

"Scared?" Claire echoed. "What was she scared of?"

"I don't know. I should go after her and see what's wrong!" Elizabeth said worriedly.

"I'm sure she'll be just fine." Claire looked deep into Elizabeth's eyes and smiled.

"Still, I really should check on her," Elizabeth insisted. After all, Julie was her friend, and if something had upset her, then Elizabeth wanted to help.

"She'll be fine," Claire repeated.

"I suppose you're right," Elizabeth said at last. "Julie really didn't seem *that* upset. It was probably nothing."

Claire reached for Elizabeth's hand. "Let's go," she said.

Reluctantly, Elizabeth followed. "I thought you might want to meet Julie," she said, glancing over her shoulder in the direction Julie had run. "Then you could have another friend."

"I have *you*, Elizabeth. And you'll be my friend forever and ever," Claire said confidently. "Would you like me to take you to some secret places today? Maybe you could write about them in your newspaper."

"That sounds like fun," Elizabeth said, brightening a little.

"Good. I know just where to start!" Claire said.

After Elizabeth had bought a lemonade, Claire led her to the fun house. The building was painted bright yellow and red, and was decorated with huge pictures of clowns. A long line of people waited to be admitted.

"Don't worry," Claire said. "We don't have to wait in line." She took Elizabeth to the back of the fun house. "This way," Claire said, opening a small door marked Private.

The room was dark, but Elizabeth could see a group of young kids who seemed to be laughing and making faces at her and Claire.

"Those children are looking into trick two-way mirrors," Claire explained. "They can only see their own reflections, but we can see through the mirrors and watch everyone."

"You mean they can't see us?" Elizabeth asked uncomfortably.

"Of course not," Claire answered.

"But don't you feel a little sneaky, watching people when they can't see you?" Elizabeth asked.

Claire shrugged. "I've gotten used to it."

Elizabeth followed Claire down a narrow, dark hallway to another two-way mirror through which they could see people trying to walk on a wobbly trick floor.

"There's a motor underneath the floor that makes it jerk back and forth," Claire explained. "If you don't hold onto the rail, you fall down."

Elizabeth recognized Caroline Pearce and Elise Jennings, two sixth-graders from Sweet Valley

Middle School, struggling to keep their balance as they crossed the unstable floor. Suddenly, Caroline fell, and as she reached out to grab her friend for support, Elise fell, too. The girls screeched with laughter.

"That looks like fun!" Elizabeth exclaimed. She took a drink of her lemonade and then offered it to Claire, but Claire waved it away. "Let's go in!" Elizabeth suggested.

Claire shook her head slowly. "It's more fun to watch, Elizabeth."

"You don't ever want to go on any of the rides, Claire. Why?"

Claire smoothed a nonexistent wrinkle in her starched cotton dress. "When the time is right, we'll go."

"What do you mean, 'when the time is right'?" Elizabeth pressed. "The carnival won't be here much longer, and I don't want to miss all the fun."

"You won't miss the fun, Elizabeth," Claire said confidently. "Not as long as you're with me." She smiled broadly and locked her dark gaze on Elizabeth.

"I suppose you're right, Claire," Elizabeth agreed.

As she took a sip on her straw, Elizabeth noticed something strange about the color of her drink.

"It's black!" she screamed in horror as she threw the cup to the ground. The black liquid splattered everywhere. Elizabeth closed her eyes in disgust—but when she opened them it had become lemonade again!

Claire clapped her hands together gleefully. "I *told* you we would have fun!"

"Fun!" Elizabeth cried. She stared at the puddle of lemonade on the floor and shuddered. "That was horrible, Claire! How did you do that?"

"It's magic, Elizabeth. Did you like it?" Claire asked.

"No!" Elizabeth snapped. She wiped a spot of lemonade off her leg. "It was awful. And you *frightened* me!"

"I did? I'm sorry, Elizabeth. I thought you wanted me to show you all my tricks." Claire's lip curled down in a pout, and Elizabeth was immediately sorry she'd yelled at Claire.

She took a deep breath to calm herself. "It's OK, Claire. It's just that I was so shocked," Elizabeth said.

"I'll get you another lemonade," Claire offered.

"No, thanks. I don't think I could stand to drink any more lemonade today," Elizabeth replied. "How did you do that, anyway? I've been to magic shows before, Claire, but I've never seen a trick like *that*!"

"Come on," Claire directed. "Let's go outside."

"Wait!" Elizabeth demanded. "At least tell me this much. How did you manage to make it look so black?"

Claire didn't answer. After a moment she repeated, "Come on, Elizabeth. Let's go outside."

Six

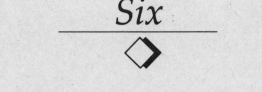

Jessica pulled Elizabeth's note off the bulletin board and scowled. "She's at the carnival *again*?"

"Guess old Madam ABC didn't scare Elizabeth off," Steven remarked through a mouthful of cereal.

"It's Mademoiselle Z, for your information." Jessica reached for the telephone. "And she put the curse on *me*, not Elizabeth."

"Think I could get a two-for-one deal?" Steven asked. "It ought to be as easy to curse two twins as it is to curse one!"

Jessica groaned and turned her back to her brother as she dialed Lila's number. "Lila?" she asked. "It's me, Jessica. I thought we could go to the mall today and get some decorations for your party."

"Aren't you going to the carnival again?" Lila inquired politely.

"Not after what happened to me yesterday," Jessica whispered. "Mademoiselle Z put a curse on me. And it was *much* worse than what she did to you!"

Behind her, Steven snickered loudly. Jessica covered her ear with her hand. "Meet me at the bus stop in half an hour, Lila," she told her friend. "I'll explain everything on the ride over."

By the time the girls had reached the mall, Jessica had told Lila all about her latest encounter with Mademoiselle Z.

"I have to admit that your curse is much worse than her prediction about me," Lila said as they strolled toward the food court in the center of the mall.

Jessica shivered. "I should have listened to you, Lila. That fortune teller has evil powers. I can't wait for the carnival to leave Sweet Valley for good!"

"Me, either," Lila agreed as the girls stopped to buy sodas. "Of course, it's too bad we have to miss all the fun stuff at the carnival. While all of our friends are having a good time, you and I have to sit around with a curse hanging over our heads. It really isn't fair."

"Wait a minute!" Jessica cried. "I've got a terrific idea! If we can't go to the carnival, let's bring the carnival to us!"

"What are you talking about, Jess?" Lila asked.

"Your New Year's Eve party," Jessica said. She dragged Lila to a table in the center of the food court. "What if we have a carnival theme? We could have games and cotton candy, and maybe even a haunted house!"

"That's a great idea!" Lila agreed. "We could even have a fortune teller!"

Jessica wasn't too sure that she wanted to have anything to do with fortune telling—even if it was fake. "Well, maybe," she said reluctantly. "I suppose we should have fortunes. After all, it *is* the start of a brand-new year. It'll be fun to predict what will happen to everyone next year."

Lila flipped her light brown hair over her shoulder. "I'll bet my father could even rent some rides. Wouldn't it be great to have our very own Ferris wheel?"

"While we're at it, we could turn your pool house into a fun house," Jessica suggested. "And instead of bumper cars, we could have bumper boats in the pool!"

Lila reached into her purse and pulled out a small notepad. "There's so much to do," she said excitedly. "Let's make a list of everything we'll need. Why don't you come back to my house?

After dinner we can start writing out the invitations. This is going to be the best party Sweet Valley Middle School has ever seen!"

They finished their sodas, and then the two of them rode the bus back to Lila's house. After dinner, they started to make invitations for the party. On each invitation Jessica drew a clown with a huge, round mouth, just like the one at the entrance to the real carnival. Inside the clown's mouth, Lila wrote:

Come one, come all!
To Lila's Carnival!
So much fun, you won't want to leave!
It's at Lila's house, on New Year's Eve!

Because Lila decided to invite almost everyone she knew, the girls didn't finish working until very late. When Jessica got home, she went straight upstairs to her bedroom, where she immediately fell fast asleep.

It was very dark when Jessica opened her eyes. She blinked and checked the blue numbers of the clock on her night table. "Two-fifteen," she groaned, rolling over and pulling the blankets up over her head. *What on earth made me wake up at this hour?* she wondered.

Then, she heard a tapping sound. She lay

very still and listened. Three loud taps, then silence. A moment later, she heard three more.

Jessica realized that she was no longer the tiniest bit sleepy. She wanted to see what had made the tapping sound, but she was far too frightened to come out from under her blanket.

She listened to the sound of the wind blowing gently outside her window. The only other sound she could hear was the loud pounding of her own heart.

The tapping came again, louder this time. Should she call for help? Elizabeth was close enough to hear her.

"I-is someone th-there?" Jessica whispered.

Then she heard the voice. It was a low, raspy man's voice, and it sounded as if it were coming from very far away.

"Stay away," the voice said.

"W-who is it?" Jessica moaned. There was a lump in her throat that kept her from shouting. Jessica's fingers shook as she slowly pulled the blanket away from her face. The familiar shadows in her room seemed to have been transformed into hideous figures, each ready to pounce on her. She heard a chattering sound and realized that it was her teeth. Then she heard the voice again.

"Stay away!" it repeated.

Jessica screamed and dove back under her covers.

A moment later the door to her room flew open, and Jessica heard the light switch flick on. She pulled down her covers and peeked out. Her father was standing in the doorway to her room, looking rumpled in his pajamas. Her mother was right behind him.

"What's the matter, honey? Did you have a bad dream?" Mr. Wakefield asked.

"There was someone tapping at my window!" Jessica cried. "And he was saying, 'Stay away'!"

Mr. Wakefield nodded. "Well, let me take a look." He walked over to Jessica's window and pulled up the shade.

Jessica shivered. She was almost too afraid to look.

"No one's out there, Jess," he said.

"But I heard someone saying, 'Stay away'!" Jessica insisted.

"It's a little windy out tonight," Mr. Wakefield said calmly. "The breeze must have blown the branches of the tree against the window and made the tapping noise. You know how close that oak tree is to the house, honey. And sometimes the wind can sound just like a person's voice."

From the hallway came Steven's drowsy voice. "What's going on?" He peeked into Jessica's room.

"Your sister just had a nightmare," Mrs. Wakefield said. "Go back to bed."

"What happened?" Elizabeth stood in the doorway of the bathroom she shared with her sister.

"Nothing!" Mrs. Wakefield repeated firmly. "Jessica had a nightmare. Now both of you, back to bed." She bent down and kissed Jessica's forehead. "Sweet dreams, honey."

When Jessica was alone again she lay perfectly still, listening carefully to the sound of the wind as it rustled the branches of the old oak tree.

It was a nightmare, she told herself. *There was nothing out there.*

But each time she closed her eyes, she remembered the eerie voice telling her to stay away. If it really had been a nightmare, she didn't ever want to fall asleep again.

Why didn't I remember to ask her where she lives? Elizabeth wondered.

She stood at the entrance to the carnival, searching the crowd for Claire. The day was overcast, and a wispy fog drifted over the grounds. The thin gray haze made faces and shapes soft and indistinct.

"Hello, Elizabeth," Claire said.

Elizabeth spun around and saw her friend standing beside a cotton-candy booth.

"Claire!" Elizabeth said in surprise. "I meant to ask you . . ."

Claire looked intently at Elizabeth, and her huge brown eyes seemed to blacken.

Elizabeth shook her head. Suddenly she felt strangely confused. "I . . . I meant to ask you something, Claire, but now . . . now I can't remember what it was."

"I'm sure it wasn't anything important," Claire said contentedly. "How would you like to play some games today, Elizabeth?"

"I'd like that," Elizabeth said, "but I don't have any tickets."

"I think you do, Elizabeth," Claire said confidently. "I'm sure you have five tickets in your jeans pocket."

"No, I just put on these jeans this morning," Elizabeth insisted.

"Check your pocket," Claire said.

Elizabeth shoved her hand into her right pocket. When she pulled it out, she was holding five red tickets!

Elizabeth stared at the tickets in disbelief. "Did you slip these in my pocket?"

Claire smiled serenely. "No, Elizabeth. They were already there."

"This is another one of your magic tricks, isn't it, Claire?" Elizabeth asked.

"Let's go to the shooting gallery," Claire suggested, as though she hadn't heard Elizabeth's question.

"Claire!" Elizabeth grabbed Claire's arm and was surprised at how thin and frail it was. "Please tell me how you do your tricks. I'd love to write about them in my *Sixers* article."

Claire's dark eyes sparkled like the ocean on a moonlit night. "You don't really want to worry about that now, do you, Elizabeth?"

"Well, sure I do—" Elizabeth began.

"Wouldn't you rather just play?" Claire asked.

Elizabeth wanted to protest. After all, the school newspaper was very important to her, and she wanted the article on the carnival to be as thorough and exciting as possible. But as soon as she opened her mouth, she found that she had nothing to say. Claire was right. She could worry about her article another time.

"That's better," Claire said in answer to Elizabeth's silence. "The shooting gallery's right around the corner."

"But I don't know how to shoot," Elizabeth argued.

"Of course you do, Elizabeth." Claire motioned for Elizabeth to follow her. "I'll help you and you'll win a great prize."

At the shooting gallery, Elizabeth handed the attendant a red ticket. He smiled at her, and Elizabeth noticed that he completely ignored Claire. But Elizabeth had gotten used to the way the employees of the carnival treated her friend. And Claire didn't seem to be bothered by their rudeness.

Elizabeth picked up a pellet rifle and examined it nervously. "I'm afraid I'll miss," she said.

"Don't worry, little lady," the attendant said kindly. "Just point it at that row of ducks and squeeze the trigger real slow."

Elizabeth aimed at the ducks and pulled the trigger. There was a loud *pop,* and the first duck fell over. "I got one!" Elizabeth cried in surprise. "I actually got one!"

She pointed the gun again and squeezed the trigger. A second duck fell over.

"Hey," the attendant said, "I thought you didn't know how to shoot!"

"I don't," Elizabeth said, mystified. She fired three more times and three more ducks fell over.

"Why don't you try for that moving squirrel way in the back?" Claire said. "That one is worth ten points."

"I can't even see it!" Elizabeth protested.

"I'll show you," Claire said as she disappeared around the side of the shooting gallery.

A moment later, Elizabeth saw Claire standing behind the various rows of targets.

She'll get hurt! Elizabeth thought desperately. "Look out!" she shouted over the deafening noise of the rifles.

"What?" the attendant asked.

"Don't worry, Elizabeth!" Claire called. "I know my way around. I'm perfectly safe here."

Pellets whizzed and targets fell all around Claire, but she didn't seem at all afraid. "Claire!" Elizabeth called urgently. "Be careful!"

"Something the matter?" the attendant asked.

"Um . . . no," Elizabeth said slowly, her eyes still fixed on Claire.

"Here's the squirrel," Claire called, pointing at a tiny wooden animal that glided by on a thin wire every few seconds. "It's worth ten points!"

"I can't even see the squirrel," Elizabeth muttered. She hesitated with her finger poised on the trigger. Her hands were cold and clammy with fear. *What if I miss?* she thought frantically.

"Come on, Elizabeth!" Claire urged.

"Get out of the way," she instructed Claire.

"I'm not *in* the way," the attendant answered, scratching his head.

"Shoot, Elizabeth!" Claire cried. "Shoot now!"

Elizabeth held her breath and slowly squeezed the trigger. Suddenly the squirrel stopped and a loud bell clanged.

"You hit the ten-pointer!" the attendant said in surprise. "You're some shot, young lady!"

Elizabeth shook her head in disbelief. How was it possible she'd hit a target she could hardly see? "Do I get a prize?" she asked in amazement.

"You get this big stuffed teddy bear," the attendant told her. "Our best prize!"

As Elizabeth reached for the bear, Claire reappeared by her side. "I can't believe I won!" Elizabeth exclaimed.

"There are lots of things people don't believe that they *should* believe, Elizabeth," Claire said with a smile.

Seven

"Look at this wonderful dress!" Jessica exclaimed.

Lila, Ellen, and Belinda were each searching through a section of The Clothes Closet, a used-clothing store in downtown Sweet Valley.

"Doesn't it look like something a star in an old movie would wear?" Jessica asked. She held up the silky blue dress for the Unicorns' inspection.

"Actually, it looks like something my grandma would wear to her garden club meeting," Ellen remarked.

Jessica sighed and returned the dress to a crowded rack.

"Aren't these shoes weird?" Belinda called from her position on the floor next to a dusty trunk. "Just look at all the buttons!" She waved a pair of high black leather shoes in the air. There were tiny buttons all the way to the top of each shoe.

"I'd rather wear my high-tops," Jessica grimaced. "I bet those shoes were really uncomfortable."

Lila put her hands on her hips. "We're not here to try on antique clothes, you guys! There are only a couple of days left until my party, and we have a ton of work to do! We're supposed to be looking for costumes for the carnival workers, not little-old-lady shoes."

"Yes, m'am!" Jessica said as she gave Lila a salute.

"Ellen, you look for outfits for the haunted house. You know, vampire or monster clothes. Belinda, you try to find stuff for the games and rides people to wear. Maybe little bow ties." Lila rubbed her palms together. "I'm going to look for a witch costume."

"She's a witch!" Jessica muttered to Belinda. Lila was getting awfully bossy about the party. She seemed to have forgotten that Jessica had spent hours helping her plan all the details!

"Who's going to run the games and rides?" Ellen asked.

"My father's hired our gardeners to help out," Lila said. "Do you and Belinda still want to be the haunted-house guides?"

"Of course!" Ellen attempted to cackle like a witch, but ended up giggling instead.

"What was that supposed to be?" Lila demanded. "A sick cat?"

"A *witch*," Ellen said defensively, her eyes flashing.

"Well, practice, will you?" Lila said. "I want everything to be just perfect. My carnival is going to be even better than the *real* carnival!"

"What about Jessica?" Ellen asked. "What's she going to do?"

Lila made a face. "Well, I think she should be our fortune teller, but she's not sure she wants to."

"Why not, Jessica?" Belinda asked.

Jessica shrugged. She wandered over to a glass case and gazed at a sparkling array of costume jewelry. It wasn't that she didn't want to be the fortune teller. But having anything to do with fortune telling seemed like a bad idea after the curse Mademoiselle Z had put on her.

"After all, Jessica has more experience with an actual fortune teller than anyone else," Lila pointed out.

"I don't have that much experience," Jessica protested. "Just a few visits to Mademoiselle Z, that's all."

"I'm beginning to think that maybe Jessica's afraid," Lila said casually as she browsed along a rack of dresses. "Maybe she thinks Mademoiselle Z won't like the competition!"

"I am *not* afraid!" Jessica said hotly. *Lila's hardly the one to talk,* she thought with annoyance. *Ever since her little spill in the mud puddle, she's been terrified of Mademoiselle Z!*

"Afraid she'll put another curse on you, Jessica?" Ellen teased.

"No, I am *not* afraid," Jessica repeated.

"Doesn't this look like Mademoiselle Z's dress?" Lila asked.

She held up a long evening dress covered with bright red sequins. They sparkled in the light like hundreds of rubies. Jessica thought it was the most beautiful dress she'd ever seen.

Lila held the dress up in front of her and gazed in the mirror admiringly. "Maybe *I'll* be the fortune teller," she murmured.

"But you said yourself that I know more about fortune telling than anyone else," Jessica said quickly.

"I suppose you're right," Lila said a bit reluctantly as she handed Jessica the dress.

Jessica held up the glittering dress and imagined herself wearing it on New Year's Eve. With that dress, she was sure to be the hit of Lila's party.

"So you'll be the fortune teller?" Lila prompted.

"What have I got to lose?" Jessica asked with a shrug. "I'm already cursed!"

*   *   *

"Jessica? Why haven't you set the table?" Mrs. Wakefield stood in the doorway to the family room, hands on hips. "I'm just about ready to serve dinner."

Jessica looked up from the TV program she was watching. "It's not my turn, Mom," she said.

"It's not?" Mrs. Wakefield asked.

"No. It's Elizabeth's turn tonight," Jessica replied.

Mrs. Wakefield pursed her lips. "Well, go upstairs and remind your sister, would you?"

Jessica trudged up the stairs. Reminding Elizabeth to do her chores felt very strange. Usually it was Jessica who needed the reminder!

She found Elizabeth sitting on the edge of her bed and gazing dreamily into the air. "Earth to Elizabeth!" Jessica said loudly.

Elizabeth turned a blank gaze toward her sister. Then she seemed to snap out of her daydream. "Hi, Jess. What's up?"

"Are you sick or something?" Jessica demanded.

Elizabeth looked surprised. "Sick? Why would you think I was sick?"

"Because the only time I've ever seen you slack off on your chores is when you're sick," Jessica explained. "Mom sent me up to get you. It's your night to set the table."

"It is?" Elizabeth asked. "Can't you do it for me?"

"Wait a minute," Jessica cried. "Who do you think you are, Elizabeth? Me?"

"OK, I'm coming." Elizabeth got slowly to her feet and followed Jessica downstairs.

All during dinner, Elizabeth seemed distracted. Steven had to ask her twice to pass the salt, and Elizabeth responded by handing him the pepper. Near the end of the meal, Jessica noticed her mother watching Elizabeth with concern.

"Elizabeth's made a new friend," Mrs. Wakefield told Mr. Wakefield. "Her parents own the carnival."

"That's funny." Mr. Wakefield looked puzzled. "I thought I read in the newspaper that the carnival was owned by some big corporation in Texas." He shrugged. "I may be wrong."

"It must be difficult for Claire, traveling with the carnival all the time," Mrs. Wakefield said to Elizabeth. "How does she manage to go to school?"

"I don't know," Elizabeth answered slowly. "I never thought to ask her."

"Maybe she has a tutor or something," Jessica offered.

"I suppose that's possible," Mrs. Wakefield said. "I imagine she misses not having a normal life—a home and friends."

"Yes." Elizabeth nodded. "She's very lonely. She says there aren't any other kids her age with the carnival."

"Does she get to go on rides and stuff for free?" Steven asked with interest.

Elizabeth shook her head. "No. I guess she's bored with all the rides, because we never go on them. We do other things."

"Well, I'll bet she would enjoy a nice home-cooked meal," Mrs. Wakefield said. "Why don't you invite her over for dinner?"

Elizabeth looked uneasy. "Um, I don't know if she can leave the carnival."

"Why not? She's probably sick to death of that stupid carnival." Jessica waited for her sister to argue, but Elizabeth just shrugged uncomfortably.

"How about New Year's Day?" Mrs. Wakefield suggested. "I believe the carnival's closed that day. And your father and I would really like to meet Claire," she added firmly.

"I'll ask her," Elizabeth agreed.

"Good. Then we'll expect her for dinner on New Year's," Mrs. Wakefield said.

"New Year's!" Jessica said suddenly. She turned to Elizabeth. "That reminds me, Elizabeth, Lila's going to have a New Year's Eve party. You're invited, of course, and I guess you could ask Claire, if you want."

"I don't really think I want to go to one of Lila's parties," Elizabeth said simply.

"Why not?" Jessica demanded.

"I just don't think it will be much fun," Elizabeth said.

"But Lila's inviting everyone from school, including all of *your* boring friends," Jessica said, a touch of annoyance in her voice. "And the theme of the party is a carnival, so Claire would feel right at home."

"Well, maybe I'll go," Elizabeth said grudgingly. "But don't count on me."

"Don't worry," Jessica grumbled. "I don't count on you for anything lately."

Late that night, Jessica woke up feeling very thirsty. Her bedside clock read 1:08 A.M. For a while she tried to fall back to sleep, but she couldn't. At last she crawled from her warm bed and headed toward the bathroom.

Jessica poured herself a glass of water and put it to her lips. And then she heard the moaning.

She looked nervously in the medicine-cabinet mirror, almost expecting to see someone standing behind her. But there was no one. Very slowly, she turned around.

The moaning noise came again—a sad, eerie sound that sent shivers down her spine. Jessica couldn't tell where it was coming from. She was sure the noise was not the tapping sound or the man's voice she had heard the other night, but it was just as horrible.

Still, she didn't want to wake up her parents. They would just tell her she was dreaming again.

"I'm not dreaming, am I?" she whispered. *How can I tell if something is real or just a dream?* she wondered.

Again she heard the noise. Jessica held her breath. It was a terrifying, low-pitched groan, like that of a wild animal. And it seemed to be getting louder by the minute!

Slowly, quietly, Jessica opened the door that led from the bathroom to Elizabeth's room. The moaning grew still louder. She opened the door wider. Moonlight was streaming in through the window, making Elizabeth's face look ghostly and pale.

"Nooo . . ." Elizabeth moaned. "Nooo . . ."

Jessica felt the hair on her neck rise in fright. Elizabeth's eyes were shut tight, and the terrible, inhuman groan was coming from her lips!

"Nooo . . . don't . . . make . . . me . . . go. . . ." Elizabeth moaned.

Eight

Elizabeth felt herself falling and falling. She felt as if she'd been falling forever.

Suddenly, she stopped. When she looked around, she found herself in the middle of a very old graveyard. A cold gray fog drifted along the ground, swirling around the crumbling tombstones.

Elizabeth shivered. She noticed that she was wearing an old-fashioned thin white dress.

Through the fog she saw a circle of brightly colored lights turning like a wheel. She was compelled to go toward the lights, but she was afraid. She reached into the pocket of her dress and pulled out a fortune cookie. The fortune said, "Beware!"

Elizabeth tried to walk away from the lights, but no matter which way she turned, they were always in front of her, growing nearer and nearer. She stopped walking altogether, but still she was moving closer to the circle of colored lights.

"No!" she cried. She tried to run, but her feet were held by the thick fog.

All at once the lights were right before her, turning in a slow circle high over her head. At her feet the fog parted, and she saw that she was standing at the edge of a freshly dug grave. At the far end of the grave was a tombstone carved with the initials *C.C.*

Elizabeth closed her eyes. When she opened them again, the writing on the tombstone had changed. Now the initials were *E.W.*

A grinning skeleton slowly rose from behind the tombstone. The skeleton turned its eyeless gaze on Elizabeth and laughed.

"Well, I declare," the skeleton shrieked. "I declare. I declare, declare, declare, declare, declare, clare, clare—"

Elizabeth screamed.

"Wake up! Wake up, Lizzie! You're having a nightmare!" a voice cried.

The skeleton wavered and disappeared. Elizabeth's eyes flew open and she sat bolt upright. "No!" she cried.

"It's OK, Lizzie." The voice was familiar.

Elizabeth blinked. "Jessica?"

"That must have been a terrible nightmare,

Elizabeth," Jessica said. "I heard you moaning all the way from my bedroom. You sounded like something in a horror movie!"

Elizabeth shook her head, trying to recall her dream, but already the images had begun to evaporate. "I guess it *was* a nightmare, but I can't remember what it was about," Elizabeth said.

"That's probably a good thing," Jessica said reassuringly.

"Sorry," Elizabeth said softly. "You can go back to sleep now."

"I'll *try*," Jessica answered. "First *I* have a nightmare, then *you* have a nightmare . . . I just wish everything would get back to normal!"

Jessica managed to fall back asleep, but not for long. She'd set her alarm to go off early, hoping to catch her sister before she left for the carnival the next morning.

"Morning, Elizabeth!" Jessica trudged into the bathroom, trying her best to sound perky. She hated getting up early—especially on a vacation day!

"Jessica!" Elizabeth exclaimed. "What are *you* doing up at this hour?"

Jessica shrugged and reached for her pink toothbrush. "You know me," she said. "Early to bed, early to rise!"

Elizabeth narrowed her eyes. "I *do* know you,

and this is definitely *not* typical Jessica Wakefield behavior!"

"You haven't exactly been acting like yourself, either," Jessica muttered as she opened the top of the toothpaste tube.

"You mean last night?" Elizabeth asked uneasily. "I'm really sorry I woke you up. The funny thing is, I still don't remember anything about the nightmare."

"Trust me, it was a whopper!" Jessica laughed, but she could tell that Elizabeth was uncomfortable. Still, she wanted to know what had been going on with her sister lately. "Doesn't it seem as if things have been a little strange around here?"

"Strange?" Elizabeth repeated.

"Well, I haven't seen you much lately," Jessica said in her best feel-sorry-for-me voice. "You're always at that silly carnival."

"You could come with me today," Elizabeth suggested. She reached for an elastic band and pulled her hair into a neat ponytail. "Claire always takes me to the most interesting places on the carnival grounds. And she knows some incredible magic tricks. You'd enjoy it."

"No way!" Jessica cried. Spending the day at the carnival was the last thing she had in mind!

"You're not still upset about that fortune teller, are you?" Elizabeth asked. "Claire says she's just a crazy old woman."

"No, I'm not afraid of her. It's just . . . well, I just think I should be careful, that's all." Jessica began brushing her teeth vigorously.

"Well, I think it's too bad that you're missing out on the fun," Elizabeth said.

Jessica rinsed out her mouth. "I have an idea, Lizzie! Why don't we go to the mall today? We could look for a skirt to go with that yellow blouse you got for Christmas. And after that we could go to Casey's for ice cream." Casey's Place, an old-fashioned ice cream parlor, was a favorite hangout for Sweet Valley Middle School students.

"I haven't been to Casey's in ages!" Elizabeth exclaimed.

For a moment, Jessica was certain she'd convinced her sister to abandon the carnival—and Claire—at least for a day. But suddenly Elizabeth's face darkened.

"No. I can't," she said, almost as though she were trying to convince herself. "I'd like to go, Jessica, but I can't. I have to spend time with Claire."

"Why?" Jessica demanded angrily. "Why do you have to be with Claire all the time?"

"She needs me," Elizabeth stated flatly.

"What about *me*?" Jessica said. "I need you, too, Lizzie!"

"But Claire's different, Jessica. She doesn't have any other friends," Elizabeth said.

"So what?" Jessica said angrily. "That's not *your* problem."

"It's only for a little while longer," Elizabeth said. Her voice was strained. "Try to understand, OK? Claire's lonely."

"So am I," Jessica muttered as she watched her sister go.

Jessica had just finished breakfast when she heard a knock at the front door.

"Are you ready to work?" Lila demanded as soon as Jessica had opened the door.

"Work?" Jessica asked.

"On my party!" Lila exclaimed. "There's hardly any time left, and we've got so much to do!" She marched into the den and collapsed dramatically on the couch. "Ellen and Belinda are over at my house already, working on the haunted house. They kept fighting over where to hang the rubber spiders. I was getting a headache, so I decided to come over here for a while."

"How does everything look so far?" Jessica wanted to know.

Lila smiled. "Amazing! You'd swear it was a real carnival! My dad rented tents for the games and food, just in case it rains. And guess what?"

"What?" Jessica asked absently. After her conversation with Elizabeth earlier, she just couldn't seem to get excited about Lila's party.

"We're actually going to have our very own Ferris wheel!" Lila said happily.

"How big is it?" Jessica stifled a yawn.

"Well, not as big as the Ferris wheel at the other carnival, of course," Lila said defensively. "But how many parties have you been to that had *any* rides at all?" She sat up and took a deep breath. "Now, what have you decided to do about the fortune telling?"

Jessica looked surprised. "What do you mean? I already have my costume."

"Have you found a crystal ball yet?" Lila asked.

Jessica rolled her eyes. "Sorry, Lila, I checked the fortune teller–supply store at the mall, but they were fresh out of crystal balls!"

Lila shook her head. "How do you plan to tell fortunes without a crystal ball? Are you planning to use a football instead?"

Jessica laughed. Actually, she hadn't given the question much thought. "Maybe we could fake it," Jessica suggested. "Use an upside-down fishbowl or something."

"Give me a break." Lila frowned. "You're supposed to be just like Mademoiselle Z."

"There's one big difference," Jessica reminded her friend. "Mademoiselle Z really *can* tell the future. I can't."

"You can pretend, can't you?" Lila

demanded. "Belinda isn't a vampire, either—at least as far as I know. But she's going to pretend to be one for the haunted house."

Jessica tried to imagine herself gazing into a crystal ball and telling each guest at Lila's party what the new year would bring. How could she ever come up with that many fortunes off the top of her head? Lila had invited practically the whole school!

"I just don't know if I can do it, Lila," she admitted. "What if I run out of predictions and start telling everybody the same thing?"

"Just tell people what you think they want to hear," Lila said, dismissing her friend's concern with a wave of her hand. "Make things up as you go along."

Jessica wasn't convinced. "Maybe I should jot down some ideas, just in case."

"Oh, great!" Lila groaned. "A fortune teller with a cheat sheet!"

Jessica ran to the kitchen and returned with a small notepad and two pencils. "This is just to get some rough ideas," she said.

Lila sighed. "My headache is getting *much* worse."

"How about, 'You will make the honor roll next semester'?" Jessica suggested.

"A little dull," Lila said.

Jessica wrote it on a slip of paper anyway. "I

know! 'You will have a very exciting love life this year.' "

"Much better!" Lila exclaimed.

Jessica quickly wrote down the fortune on another piece of paper. But after a few minutes, the girls seemed to run out of good ideas.

"Let's see," Jessica said, tapping her pencil on the coffee table. "We've done grades, love, money, travel . . . maybe we should have some bad fortunes, too. Like, 'You will flunk out of school.' "

"No," Lila said firmly. "I think we should have only happy fortunes." She frowned. "You were right. Coming up with fortunes is much harder than I thought it would be."

"We could go further into the future," Jessica pointed out. " 'You will marry a millionaire.' Or, 'You will become a movie star.' "

"Good idea!" Lila nodded. "Then we can make up anything we want, as long as it's positive."

Jessica frowned at the growing pile of fortunes. "I'll never remember all of these," she said. Suddenly she thought of the fortune cookies at the Red Dragon Restaurant. "I've got an idea! What if we just fold up these pieces of paper and I pick one out of a jar to read to each guest? It's not exactly how Mademoiselle Z does it, but at least I won't have to memorize hundreds of fortunes! We could do one jar for boys and one jar for girls."

"Well, all right," Lila agreed reluctantly. "I guess it's better than nothing."

"What should I call myself?" Jessica asked as she began to fold the fortunes into small squares. "The name should sound exotic and mysterious, like Mademoiselle Z."

"How about Mademoiselle F?" Steven suggested from the door of the den. "*F* for *fake*." He laughed loudly, but Jessica and Lila weren't amused.

"Hey, Mademoiselle F!" Steve went on. "Can *you* put curses on people, too?"

"If I could," Jessica called back, "you'd be the world's most hideous toad."

"The fog is very thick today, isn't it, Elizabeth?" Claire pointed toward the beach, where a thick gray blanket of fog hid the ocean from view.

Elizabeth nodded. "It's strange," she said. "It's hardly ever foggy in Sweet Valley."

The girls continued strolling along the edge of the carnival grounds. "Is something wrong, Elizabeth?" Claire asked.

Elizabeth frowned. "I was trying to remember something—something my mother said to me. But I just can't seem to recall what it was."

Claire smiled, her luminous dark eyes fixed on Elizabeth. "I'm sure it wasn't important."

Elizabeth looked toward the ocean again, and all at once she remembered that her mother had asked her to invite Claire to dinner!

"Why are you looking away, Elizabeth?" Claire asked quickly. "Are you trying to be mean to me?"

"No," Elizabeth said in surprise, turning back to face Claire. "I just remembered that my mom wanted me to invite you to dinner."

"Your mother must be very nice," Claire said coldly. "But I can't leave the carnival."

"Why not?" Elizabeth asked. She searched Claire's eyes for a hint of her reason.

"Why not *what*, Elizabeth?" Claire stared at her.

"Why not . . . um," Elizabeth began. "Why not . . . why . . . why don't we go and play?"

"Yes! Let's go and play!" Claire clapped her hands happily.

As they walked back toward the center of the carnival, Elizabeth tried to think about what had happened in the last few minutes. But somehow it was already just a blur. Lately, she had been finding that all sorts of things just seemed to evaporate from her memory.

"I'm so glad we're best friends, Elizabeth,"

Claire said as the girls headed toward the food booths.

"You're a friend to no one!" a voice cried.

Elizabeth looked up in surprise to see a tall woman in a red dress covered with mirrored beads standing directly in front of them.

"Get out of my way, you crazy old woman!" Claire snapped angrily.

The woman tried to look defiantly at the little girl, but Elizabeth could see the fear in her eyes.

"You cannot do this, Claire!" the woman said firmly.

"I can do anything I want!" Claire responded. "I'm the owner's daughter and I can do anything I want to do! Anything! And you know what happens to people who try to stop me, don't you?"

The woman in the red dress took a step backward. "You . . . you don't scare me." Her voice was shaky.

"Oh, yes I do," Claire said calmly. "Now stay out of my way. My friend and I are playing."

The woman fell back and Claire led Elizabeth past.

"What was *that* all about?" Elizabeth demanded. Claire had seemed so angry and threatening!

Claire shrugged. "That? Oh, she's the crazy woman we saw before—"

"The fortune teller. I remember," Elizabeth interrupted.

"She's not a fortune teller. She's just a phony." Claire laughed scornfully. "She's been with the carnival ever since she was a little girl, so my father doesn't want to fire her." Claire looked at Elizabeth and grinned. "Of course, that doesn't mean I'm going to let her go around being nasty to me and my friend."

"Are you sure she's really crazy?" Elizabeth asked uneasily.

"Don't worry about it anymore," Claire reassured her. "As long as you're with me, Elizabeth, you'll always be safe."

Nine

Jessica applied an extra coat of bright red nail polish to her thumbnail. Though her nails were much shorter than Mademoiselle Z's, they were going to be just as red!

"Dry, will you?" she muttered, blowing on her fingernails as hard as she could.

Jessica walked over to the full-length mirror in her bedroom and smiled at her reflection. The red sequined dress shimmered as she moved. It was a little too big for her, and a few sequins were missing, but the overall effect was still very nice.

Jessica stepped carefully into the shiny red high heels Lila had found for her at the used-clothing store. They were also too big, but if she walked carefully, her ankles hardly wobbled at all.

Jessica made her way to the top of the staircase and called out, "Ladies and gentlemen! Presenting the amazing Mademoiselle J!"

Mr. and Mrs. Wakefield appeared at the foot of the stairs, with Steven close behind. "You look amazing, all right!" Steven said, shaking his head.

As Jessica reached the last two steps, her left foot slipped out of her shoe and she toppled. Just in the nick of time, she grabbed the railing for support. "Stupid shoes! I *told* Lila they were too big."

"We can stuff some tissues in the toes so they'll fit better," Mrs. Wakefield suggested as she retrieved Jessica's shoe.

"Since you can see the future, Mademoiselle J, I suppose you knew all along that you were going to trip," Steven teased.

"All right, Steven, that's enough," Mr. Wakefield warned. "I think your sister looks very mysterious—not to mention very pretty. Just like a real fortune teller."

"What time does the party start?" Mrs. Wakefield asked.

"Eight o'clock," Jessica said. "But I'm supposed to get to Lila's early to help with any last-minute problems."

"Are you sure you don't want some dinner before you go?" Mrs. Wakefield asked as the family walked to the kitchen.

"Are you kidding? Lila's going to have enough

food to feed the entire school!" Jessica glanced anxiously at the clock in the kitchen. "I just wish Elizabeth would come home from the carnival so we could get going."

Mr. Wakefield went to the stove to stir a pot of his special homemade chili. "What do you know about this new friend of Elizabeth's?" he asked.

Jessica shrugged. "Just what Elizabeth has told me. I've never actually met her."

"I'll feel much better after we meet her tomorrow," Mrs. Wakefield said.

"I'll feel much better when Elizabeth starts acting normal again. She's been—" Jessica paused as she heard the front door open.

"Anybody home?" Elizabeth called from the living room.

"In the kitchen, dear!" Mrs. Wakefield answered.

"Hi, everybody," Elizabeth said dully as she came into the kitchen. "What's going on?"

"Where have you *been?*" Jessica demanded. "Did you forget about Lila's New Year's Eve party?"

"Lila's what?" Elizabeth sat down heavily at the kitchen table. She looked very tired. "Oh, that's right. It's New Year's Eve, isn't it?"

"Do you feel all right, honey?" Mrs. Wakefield asked. She placed her palm on Elizabeth's forehead. "You don't seem to have a temperature."

"I feel fine," Elizabeth protested. "Why is everybody looking at me so strangely?"

"Maybe you should stay home tonight," Mrs. Wakefield suggested.

"Good." Elizabeth nodded. "I really didn't want to go to Lila's, anyway."

"I don't know, Alice." Mr. Wakefield gave his wife a meaningful look. "Maybe it would be a good idea for Elizabeth to be with some of her other friends. Have you seen Amy since Christmas vacation started, Elizabeth?"

"No, not really," Elizabeth confessed. "But I've been so busy with Claire—"

"I think your father's right," Mrs. Wakefield interrupted. "Lila's party might be just what the doctor ordered."

Elizabeth shrugged. "Whatever you say."

"Great!" Jessica said with relief. "You won't be sorry, Elizabeth."

"I'll just go change my clothes." When Elizabeth reached the doorway, she paused. "By the way, Jessica," she said slowly. "Is that a new dress? I don't think I've ever seen you wear it before."

Jessica didn't join in her family's laughter. She wasn't entirely sure that her sister had been joking.

* * *

A half-hour later, Mr. Wakefield dropped the twins off in front of Lila's house. "This place always makes me uncomfortable," Elizabeth whispered to Jessica as they followed a servant through the main foyer.

"Everything's so *big* here," Elizabeth continued. "It's weird."

"If you think this is weird," Jessica whispered back, "wait until you see what they've done to the backyard!"

"Jessica! I was beginning to get worried!" Lila appeared at the top of the grand staircase. She was wearing a long, white, flowing gown covered with sequins. On her head was a pointed white hat, and in her hand she held a magic wand topped off with a gold star.

"I thought you were going to dress as a witch," Jessica protested.

"Haven't you ever heard of a good witch?" Lila pirouetted to show off her dress.

"But all of the Unicorns were supposed to dress like people from the carnival," Jessica argued. "The only witch at the carnival is the one from the haunted house, and you don't look anything like her!"

"Well, wait until you see Ellen and Belinda. They look very realistic. But after all, I'm the hostess of the party. *I* have to look beautiful." Lila smiled.

"Was I supposed to wear a costume?" Elizabeth asked in confusion.

"No," Jessica said. "Only the Unicorns are wearing costumes. Lila was *supposed* to dress like the witch from the haunted house, but she looks more like the prom queen from the Land of Oz High School!"

Lila led the twins through several elegantly furnished rooms until they came to a set of sliding glass doors. The girls stepped onto a broad patio, and Elizabeth and Jessica gasped in amazement.

"It looks just like the real carnival!" Elizabeth was transfixed.

"It looks *better* than the real carnival!" Jessica exclaimed. "So much newer and cleaner than that old place. And there's no Mademoiselle Z around to put curses on people."

All of the trees on the Fowler's huge lawn sparkled with colored lights, and even the formal boxwood garden had been lit. Merry organ music filled the air, and brightly colored tents had been set up in the center of the grounds.

"My father had people working on this until late last night," Lila explained as she reached up to adjust her tall, pointed hat. "Boy, is this thing hard to keep on straight!" she muttered. "Come on, I'll give you a tour."

The girls first stopped by the giant in-ground swimming pool. Little motorized boats, their sides protected by rubber inner tubes, bobbed in the water. "These are the bumper boats," Lila said. "And those yellow tents over there are all game booths. We have darts, a ring-toss game, and a shooting gallery."

"A shooting gallery?" Elizabeth echoed.

"It's just two popguns and some paper targets," Lila explained. "But the prizes are just as good as those at the real carnival!"

"What's in the orange tents?" Jessica asked excitedly.

"Food! There's cotton candy, hot dogs, caramel corn—you name it!" Lila replied proudly.

"Great! I'm starving!" Jessica said. "Aren't you, Elizabeth?"

Elizabeth shrugged. She was much more interested in the Ferris wheel at the edge of the Fowler property.

"It's small, but it's still a real Ferris wheel," Lila said. "I wish my father hadn't rented that stupid merry-go-round, though. I haven't been on one of those since I was a little kid! At least the band will start playing soon and we won't have to listen to that dopey organ music."

"Let's go see the haunted house," Jessica suggested.

"We're using the pool house for that." Lila

pointed to a small building on the far side of the pool. Black cloth covered all of the windows, and strange howls and moans could be heard coming through the doorway.

"Ellen found a tape recording called *Halloween Spookhouse*," Lila explained as she led the twins toward the entrance. "We're going to play it all night long because Ellen has the dumbest witch's cackle I've ever heard."

As if on cue, Ellen popped out of the door-way. She was carrying a broom and wearing a long black gown that Jessica recognized from the antique-clothing store. "Welcome to my haunted house!" she cried. "I hope you have a frightful visit!"

"Save it, Ellen," Lila said with a wave of her hand. "It's just us. And where's your mask, anyway?"

"Ellen doesn't *need* a mask!" Belinda called. She emerged from the pool house wearing a very convincing vampire costume, complete with fake pointed teeth.

"Very funny, Belinda," Ellen retorted. "Have you ever thought about braces?"

"Cut it out, you two," Lila commanded. "Let's show the twins the inside of the haunted house."

Rubber spiders and glow-in-the-dark plastic skeletons hung from the ceiling of the cramped pool house. In one corner of the room sat a long cardboard box painted to look like a coffin. Jessica thought that the entire setup could hardly compare to the haunted house at the real carnival. But she was a little surprised to see that her twin actually looked uncomfortable.

"Here," Ellen said in her witch voice. "Stick your hand in this, my pretties!" She held out a large bowl filled with something gooey.

"Yuck." Jessica made a face. "What *is* that stuff?"

"Human eyeballs!" Ellen tried again to cackle.

"They look like grapes to me," Jessica remarked casually. "In goopy red Jell-O."

"Olives, actually," Ellen said. "We tried grapes, but olives felt more disgusting."

"Well, you guys get the general idea," Lila said. "We have a big piece of raw liver that's supposed to be a human heart, and a falling sword made out of tinfoil." She shrugged. "The usual."

Just as the girls turned to leave, a horrible scream filled the air. Jessica and Elizabeth spun around to see a white-faced boy climbing out of the coffin.

"Wait a minute!" Jessica laughed. "That's Ellen's little brother, Mark! For a second, you actually had me scared!" Jessica suddenly became aware of Elizabeth's hand on her arm. Her sister's face was almost as pale as Mark's.

"Elizabeth!" Jessica tried to pry Elizabeth's fingers loose. "Lighten up! It was just a trick!" When they were outside again and away from the others, she took Elizabeth's hand. "Are you OK?"

Elizabeth pulled her hand away and rubbed her eyes. "I'm fine. It's just . . ."

"Just what?" Jessica prompted.

"Nothing," Elizabeth said, shaking her head. "Claire does lots of tricks, too. Sometimes they kind of scare me, but she says it's silly to be scared by a trick. It *is* silly to be scared by a trick, isn't it?"

Jessica looked at her twin. "I guess that depends on what the trick is, Elizabeth."

"Jessica! Elizabeth!" Lila called. "You haven't seen the grand finale!"

"I hope it's more grand than the haunted house," Jessica whispered. She was relieved to see that Elizabeth almost smiled.

Lila led them to a small table and chair that had been set up in the center of the lawn. The table was draped in a gold cloth, and a hand-lettered sign taped to it said, THE AMAZING MADE-MOISELLE J! KNOW YOUR FUTURE NOW! ALL FORTUNES GUARANTEED OR YOUR MONEY BACK!

"But we're not charging anything, Lila," Jessica pointed out.

"That's why the fortunes are guaranteed!" Lila laughed. "I thought we would wait until it's almost midnight, and then bring out the fortunes for you to read. That way everyone can hear them."

"She hates Claire," Elizabeth said suddenly.

"Who?" Jessica looked at her sister with a puzzled expression.

"The fortune teller," Elizabeth said. "But Claire says she's crazy."

"Well, then, I guess Claire can't be *all* bad," Jessica said.

But Elizabeth had turned away from her sister. "There's the shooting gallery," she said. "Let's go. I'm a very good shot."

Elizabeth was surprised that she didn't hit any of the targets in the shooting gallery. However, Jessica had managed to win a pair of purple sunglasses after only a few tries. Lila had made sure that there would be lots of purple prizes for all of her Unicorn friends. Purple was their favorite color.

By then the party was in full swing. Elizabeth was surrounded by familiar faces, but she could see only Claire's face, her eyes shiny with tears.

Is Claire unhappy right now? Elizabeth wondered as she strolled past a line of kids waiting impatiently for cotton candy. *Is she mad because I can't be with her tonight?*

"Hi, Elizabeth!" Elizabeth heard someone call

her name, but she kept walking. The voices and the music from the band seemed to her to blur together into one soft, rushing noise, like the sound of the ocean.

"Elizabeth!" Amy cried again. "Have you gone deaf or something?"

It took Elizabeth a moment to recognize her friend. "Hi, Amy," Elizabeth said in a voice that lacked all expression.

"I called your name three times!" Amy said.

Elizabeth felt a sudden wave of sadness. Amy's face seemed so familiar and kind! "I'm sorry about our bike ride the other day, Amy," she said softly. "I guess I just forgot."

"That's OK." Amy shrugged. "No big deal."

"I've been busy at the carnival—" Elizabeth began.

"Jessica said you've made a new friend there," Amy interrupted. "Claire? Is that her name?"

"Yes." Elizabeth nodded slowly. "Claire." As she looked at her friend's face again, Claire's sad brown eyes, dark with loneliness and resentment, stared back at her.

"Well, anyway," Amy said, "I've been wanting to talk to you about my research for the article on the carnival."

"Article?" Elizabeth repeated.

"For the *Sixers*," Amy sounded frustrated. "We've already discussed it once."

"Oh." Elizabeth didn't sound very interested.

"I think you should listen to what I've learned so far—" Amy persisted.

Elizabeth began to walk away.

"Elizabeth?" Amy grabbed her friend's arm. "What's wrong?"

"Nothing's wrong, Claire," Elizabeth said dully.

"I'm not Claire, I'm Amy! Whatever's wrong, you can tell me! We always tell each other everything!" Amy cried.

Elizabeth shook her head. "There's nothing wrong, Amy. Nothing at all."

Jessica hopped off the tiny Ferris wheel and was surprised to find Amy Sutton waiting for her.

"Jessica, we have to talk!" Amy insisted.

"Sure, Amy." One look at Amy's face told Jessica all she needed to know. "This is about Elizabeth, isn't it?"

Amy nodded solemnly. "I'm really starting to worry about her," she said. "She's just not acting like herself."

"I know." Jessica sighed heavily. "She's been acting really weird since she started spending all her time at the carnival."

"Do you think it could have something to do with this new friend of hers?" Amy asked.

Jessica rolled her eyes. "How should I know? I've never even met the girl."

"Jessica!" Lila called from the patio by the pool. "It's time to do the fortunes."

"Sorry, Amy," Jessica apologized. "I've got to go be a fortune teller. Anyway, the carnival will be leaving Sweet Valley in a few more days. And then Elizabeth will be normal again."

"I hope you're right, Jessica," Amy said doubtfully. "But do me a favor, will you?"

"Sure. What?" Jessica wanted to know.

"Make sure you predict good things for your sister, OK?" Amy shook her head. "I have the feeling she can use all the help she can get."

Ten

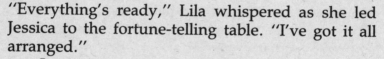

"Everything's ready," Lila whispered as she led Jessica to the fortune-telling table. "I've got it all arranged."

Jessica sat down at the table. "Ouch," she muttered. "My knee hit something."

"Shh! Those are the fortunes!" Lila carefully lifted the gold tablecloth. On a small stand were the two round bowls they had labeled at the Wakefields' the other afternoon. One was marked *B* for *boys*, and one was marked *G* for *girls*.

"This way, you can just reach into the appropriate bowl, and no one will know you're faking it!" Lila explained.

"That's not how we planned it, Lila!" Jessica protested.

"But this way you'll seem like a *real* fortune

teller!" Lila insisted. "Just lower your head, read the piece of paper, and look up. It'll work, I promise!"

"I don't know," Jessica said doubtfully.

"Trust me," Lila assured her. "By the way, I kept all the fortunes hidden away in my closet until tonight so that no one could sneak a peek." She rubbed her hands together. "Are you ready for your big moment?"

"As ready as I'll ever be," Jessica said, smoothing her hair.

Lila asked the band to stop playing and stepped up to the microphone. "Attention, everyone!" she said, pausing to clear her throat. "I am proud to present the amazing Mademoiselle J, who will use her remarkable powers to predict the future of each and every one of you! Please step up to the table in the center of the lawn."

Jessica tapped her red fingernails nervously on the table. But as the crowd started to gather around her, she began to feel better. After all, Jessica loved being the center of attention. And who knew more about fortune tellers than she did?

"Hey, Mademoiselle!" a voice called. "Who's going to win the Super Bowl this year?"

Jessica looked over to see Bruce Patman, one of the cutest guys in the seventh grade, grinning at her. "Well?" he asked.

"Do not disturb Mademoiselle J when she is trying to concentrate," Jessica warned in a low, whispery voice that sounded like Mademoiselle Z. She closed her eyes and put her fingers on her temples. "Step forward, young man."

"Who, me?" Bruce asked. Two of his friends pushed him toward Jessica's table.

"What is your name, young man?" Jessica asked.

"You already *know* my name," Bruce replied. "And I hate to break it to you, but you're really Jessica Wakefield, not Mademoiselle J!"

The kids began to laugh. "Silence!" Jessica commanded.

Just then, a few fast-moving clouds hid the moon from view. The crowd fell silent. "Wow," someone said. "Not bad, Jessica!"

Jessica lowered her head and began to sway back and forth, just as Mademoiselle Z had done. Carefully she reached under the tablecloth, pulled out a slip of paper from the jar marked *B*, and opened it in her lap. Just as Lila had predicted, no one could see what she was doing. Unfortunately, it was so dark that Jessica could barely read the fortune.

"You will, uh . . . you will be quarterback of your high school football team," Jessica whispered in her best Mademoiselle Z voice.

"All right!" Bruce cried. He stepped back into the crowd, looking very pleased with himself.

"Next?" Jessica asked. "Who will be next?"

To her surprise, several people volunteered. It didn't seem to matter whether or not she could *really* see into the future. Everybody just wanted to hear a happy prediction—even if the prediction didn't make much sense. Caroline Pearce, who couldn't even carry a tune, was thrilled to learn that she would soon be a famous rock star.

Some fortunes seemed to be just right. Brooke Dennis, whose father was a famous Hollywood screenwriter, was told that she would be a big movie star. And Randy Mason, who was already the president of the sixth-grade class, was not very surprised to learn that he would one day be a powerful politician.

Finally, Amy pushed Elizabeth forward. "Do Elizabeth Wakefield, Mademoiselle J," she said.

Jessica stared sadly at her twin sister, who stood before her looking dazed and uninterested. Without bothering to pull out one of the slips, Jessica spoke softly. "You will soon learn the value of your *true* friends."

For a moment, Elizabeth's eyes seemed to glisten with tears. Then she turned and walked away.

"Last, but not least!" Lila said, quickly taking Elizabeth's place. "Do me, Mademoiselle J!"

"But, Lila!" Jessica whispered. "Why bother?"

"Because I've been keeping track, and the only fortune left is the one that says, 'You will be a famous model'!"

"Oh, all right," Jessica muttered. She gazed toward the far end of the yard, where Elizabeth was walking all by herself.

Jessica pulled the last slip of paper from the bowl marked G. " 'You will soon go completely bald.' " The words were out of Jessica's mouth before she realized what she had said.

"What?" Lila gasped. "We didn't write that!"

"You said the fortunes were hidden away," Jessica hissed. "How could this have gotten in with the others?"

"If I didn't write it, and you didn't write it, then who did?" Lila's eyes were wide with fear. She reached up to touch her hair protectively.

"I don't know," Jessica said excitedly. "But I *knew* something would go wrong if we made fun of Mademoiselle Z!"

The New Year's Eve party had made Elizabeth very tired, and she had slept late the next morning. *I hope Claire's not worried about me*, she thought to herself as she walked slowly downstairs. Claire seemed to get cranky if Elizabeth wasn't at the carnival first thing in the morning.

"Where are you going?" Jessica asked as Elizabeth approached the front door.

"I'm on my way to the carnival," Elizabeth said.

Jessica shook her head. "Not today, Elizabeth. It's closed for New Year's Day. Don't you remember?"

Elizabeth frowned. Was it true that the carnival was closed that day? She didn't think that Claire had ever mentioned it. "Are you sure?" Elizabeth asked.

"Of course I'm sure," Jessica said. "Just about everything's closed today—even the mall."

"But—but how will I get in to see Claire?" Elizabeth asked anxiously. "She'll be so lonely if I don't go see her."

"Well, too bad!" Jessica was exasperated. "She'll just have to find something else to do today."

"But you don't understand!" Elizabeth cried. "I *have* to see Claire. I *have* to see her every day!" *Why doesn't Jessica understand?* Elizabeth thought. *Claire needs me.*

"You sound like some kind of robot, Lizzie!" Jessica said angrily. "All you do is spend time with Claire! All you talk about is Claire! It's as if Claire were taking over your mind."

Taking over my mind? Elizabeth wondered. *What a silly thought.* But for a moment she felt anxious. She *was* spending an awful lot of time with Claire. Still, Claire was so nice.

Or was she? Elizabeth remembered Claire's harsh words to Mademoiselle Z. If Claire was so nice, why was Mademoiselle Z so afraid of her? And why did all the workers at the carnival act as if she wasn't even there?

It bothered Elizabeth to think that way about Claire. Without meaning to do so, Elizabeth pictured Claire's deep, dark eyes and her sad, faraway smile, and all of a sudden, her doubts vanished.

"OK," Jessica said, "give me the silent treatment if you want, Elizabeth. But I'm telling you, you'd better watch out if you want to have any friends left after the carnival leaves!"

Elizabeth watched her sister storm away. Briefly she considered trying to make up with Jessica, but she didn't know what to say. Besides, Jessica wasn't the real problem. The *real* problem was that she was going to have to spend the whole day without Claire!

"Elizabeth!" Mrs. Wakefield smiled at her daughter. "Do you know if there's anything special your friend Claire would like for dinner?"

"Dinner?" Elizabeth echoed.

"Yes. You *did* invite her, didn't you?" her mother asked.

Elizabeth searched her memory. She vaguely

remembered having asked Claire to come for dinner, but she couldn't remember Claire's response at all. "Yes." Elizabeth nodded at last. "I asked her."

"Good," Mrs. Wakefield said. "I thought about making a roast. Do you think she would like that?"

Elizabeth shrugged. "I guess so, Mom."

Mrs. Wakefield peered closely at Elizabeth. "Are you all right, honey? You're not coming down with something, are you?" She pursed her lips. "Maybe your father and I shouldn't have let you go to Lila's party last night."

"I'm fine," Elizabeth responded. She tried to smile.

"I think you'd better stay inside today," Mrs. Wakefield said. "You may have a touch of the flu."

"I'm fine," Elizabeth repeated quietly. *Why is everyone treating me so strangely?* she wondered. *It just doesn't make sense!*

At least she would get to see Claire that evening. Elizabeth tried to imagine her friend sitting at the dinner table, talking with the family and eating roast beef. But somehow it was very hard for Elizabeth to picture Claire ever doing such a normal and everyday thing.

"When's dinner?" Steven asked, rubbing his stomach. "I'm starved."

Mrs. Wakefield was bending over the open oven door, testing the roast with a long-handled fork. "Whenever Elizabeth's friend shows up."

"Well, I hope that's *soon*," Steven grumbled.

"Me, too," Mrs. Wakefield muttered. "This roast is going to be completely dried out if I have to leave it in the oven much longer."

"Elizabeth!" Steven yelled. "Where's your dumb friend?"

"She has a name!" Elizabeth answered as she entered the kitchen.

"All right, then," Steven said impatiently. "Where's your dumb friend *Claire*? I'm going to starve to death!"

"I don't know," Elizabeth admitted.

"Are you sure she's coming?" Mrs. Wakefield asked.

Elizabeth nodded. She was almost positive that Claire had promised to come. But it was so hard to remember their conversations.

"Honey, is dinner about ready?" Mr. Wakefield asked as he joined the family.

"Dinner was ready an hour ago." Mrs. Wakefield sighed and turned to Elizabeth. "I'm sorry, Elizabeth, but we can't wait for Claire any longer. Why don't you call her and see if you can find out what's going on."

"I don't know her number," Elizabeth said

miserably. "But I'm sure she'll come if we just wait."

"Well, if she does, she'll be welcome to join us," Mrs. Wakefield said firmly.

At last the family sat down to eat. Elizabeth tried to hide her disappointment about Claire, but she could barely touch her food.

"You know, Elizabeth, Claire could have at least called to tell you she couldn't make it," Jessica remarked. "How could she be so rude?"

"Jessica," Mr. Wakefield said, "don't provoke your sister. I'm sure she feels bad enough." He smiled kindly at Elizabeth. "I am disappointed that Claire didn't show up, though. Your mother and I like to meet your friends. Now I'm not so sure that you should continue to see Claire."

"What?" Elizabeth cried in disbelief.

"We're not trying to be unfair, Elizabeth," Mrs. Wakefield said gently, "but we'd feel better if we at least had had the chance to meet her."

"And to see if you approve of her!" Elizabeth added accusingly.

Mr. Wakefield sighed. "We've never had any reason to doubt your choice of friends before, Elizabeth, and we're not saying that you can't ever see Claire again. But we want to meet her."

"You all act as if she's some kind of monster or something!" Elizabeth said hotly.

"I didn't say that," Mr. Wakefield said. "If

she's as nice as you say she is, I'm sure we'll all like Claire as much as you do."

"I doubt it," Jessica muttered.

"Why don't we change the subject?" Mrs. Wakefield suggested brightly. "Has anyone made any New Year's resolutions?"

Elizabeth stared sullenly at her plate. She'd already made one resolution—to see Claire again, no matter what her parents said.

"Elizabeth, your father and I told you last night, the answer is no!"

Jessica woke the next morning to the sound of her mother's voice in the hallway. She jumped out of bed and put her ear to her door. Her mother definitely did not sound happy—and neither did Elizabeth.

"But I have to see Claire!" Elizabeth cried.

Jessica shook her head in amazement. She couldn't remember ever hearing Elizabeth argue with their mother!

"The only thing you *have* to do is clean up your room!" Mrs. Wakefield answered sternly.

Jessica waited to hear Elizabeth's response, but the argument appeared to be over. She opened the door cautiously and peeked outside. The hallway was empty.

"Great way to wake up!" Jessica muttered to

herself. She dressed quickly and went downstairs for breakfast.

"Hi, honey." Mrs. Wakefield seemed unhappy. "I guess you heard me arguing with Elizabeth. I'm sorry. I've never seen her act so strange before. It worries me, and I lost my temper."

"I understand, Mom," Jessica answered. "She *has* been awfully hard to talk to lately."

Just then there was a knock at the front door. "I'll get it," Jessica said.

Amy Sutton stood on the front porch, a loose-leaf notebook in her hand. "Hi, Amy," Jessica said.

"Hi, Jessica," Amy said. "Is Elizabeth home?"

"Elizabeth!" Jessica called. "Amy's here!" She lowered her voice to a whisper. "I'm glad you're here, Amy. Maybe you can get Elizabeth to snap out of her weird mood."

Amy nodded toward the top of the stairs, where Elizabeth had just appeared. "Hi, Elizabeth," she said.

"What do you want?" Elizabeth snapped.

Amy's face grew flushed. "I—I wanted you to come with me to interview a man for our story about the carnival," Amy stammered.

"Well, I don't want to," Elizabeth retorted.

"But it's for the *Sixers*—" Amy began.

"Who cares about the *Sixers*?" Elizabeth said. "Do whatever you want—just leave me alone."

Jessica and Amy watched in disbelief as Elizabeth turned away.

"That does it!" Jessica vowed. "Amy, we're going to find out what's at the bottom of this, once and for all!"

Eleven

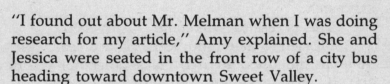

"I found out about Mr. Melman when I was doing research for my article," Amy explained. She and Jessica were seated in the front row of a city bus heading toward downtown Sweet Valley.

"Who's Mr. Melman?" Jessica asked.

"He's the man who designed the haunted house at the carnival," Amy said. "I thought he might be able to tell us something interesting about the carnival—like why it was forced to leave those two other towns in the northern part of the state. Oh, this is our stop, Jessica."

The girls climbed off the bus in front of a shabby-looking five-story office building.

"This way," Amy said. "His office is on the third floor."

After climbing three steep flights of stairs,

they came to a frosted glass door with the name *Alan J. Melman* stenciled on it. Amy knocked, and a man's voice called, "Come on in."

Mr. Melman, a man in his sixties with a fringe of gray hair, was sitting behind a desk, eating a huge, sloppy sandwich.

"Hello, young ladies," he said. "What can I do for you?"

"I'm Amy Sutton," Amy said. "I'm a reporter for our class newspaper. You remember, I called you and made an appointment?"

"So you did." Mr. Melman put down his sandwich.

"This is Jessica Wakefield," Amy said.

"Pleased to meet you both. Have a seat." Mr. Melman motioned to two cracked leather chairs and the girls sat down. "Now, if I remember correctly, you wanted to know something about the old days, when I designed attractions for carnivals."

"Actually, we were wondering about a particular carnival," Amy said. "We wanted to know about—"

"The carnival that's here in town?" Mr. Melman interrupted, his expression serious.

"Yes, sir. That's the carnival," Amy replied. "I read in an old newspaper that you had designed the haunted house."

Mr. Melman wiped his hands on a napkin.

"Yes, I did that job. It was about ten years ago, when the carnival was over near Sacramento. At the time, the carnival had a haunted house that must have been fifty years old. It's a wonder it hadn't burned down sooner."

"Burned down?" Jessica asked.

"Yep, it burned to the ground one night." Mr. Melman leaned back in his chair. "There were a lot of rumors. Folks said a local family was responsible. There was some long, confused story about the family's son having been driven crazy. It seems they figured the haunted house had had something to do with it." He shook his head. "I never did get the whole story straight."

"So then the carnival asked you to build a new haunted house?" Amy prompted.

"Yes, I got the contract," Mr. Melman said. "I showed them some ideas. They liked the ideas—or at least they liked my low prices. You know how these corporations are, always watching every penny."

"Corporation?" Jessica sat up straighter in her chair. "Isn't the carnival owned by a family?"

Mr. Melman rubbed his chin. "Well, I don't exactly remember all the details. It's been ten years, after all. But I could have sworn the carnival was owned by some big company down in Texas."

"That's just what my dad read in the newspaper!" Jessica confirmed.

"Anyway, I got the job," Mr. Melman continued. "I was mighty glad at the time, because I needed the work. But later . . ."

"Later?" Amy encouraged him.

"Well, later I began to wonder about the place." Mr. Melman smiled. "You're going to think I'm a crazy old man, but as I worked on the place, I began to get a scary feeling." He laughed. "Silly, isn't it? I design a place to scare little kids and it ends up scaring me."

"What, exactly, scared you?" Amy asked, writing as fast as she could in her notebook.

Mr. Melman hesitated. "Well, you know that haunted houses are supposed to be just fun. Something jumps out at you and you squeal. There's nothing really mean or terrifying about them. But while I worked on *that* haunted house, I began to feel that the place was changing."

"Changing how?" Jessica asked.

Mr. Melman looked right into Jessica's eyes. "It felt as if something horrible, something *evil* had moved in there."

Jessica felt a chill go up her spine. She looked over at Amy. Her face was very pale.

"But if it had just been the feeling, well, I guess I could have handled that," Mr. Melman went on.

"Was there something else?" Jessica asked. "Something *more* than a feeling?"

Mr. Melman nodded. "Yes. There was the tombstone." He cocked his head to one side. "Did either of you two go through the haunted house?"

"I did," Jessica answered.

Mr. Melman nodded grimly. "Then you'll remember that I designed the house to split into two different rooms. One was built around a vampire theme—"

"That's the path I took," Jessica interrupted.

"Well, then you missed the worst of it." Mr. Melman clenched his hands together. "The ghost room was the last part of the house I worked on. The room ends with a sort of open grave you have to pass through. Over the grave I built a tombstone of wood and covered it with fake moss. I had carved R.I.P. on the tombstone. You know—it stands for rest in peace."

Mr. Melman fell silent for a moment. He seemed to be thinking back, trying to remember every detail. At last he spoke in a harsh whisper. "To this day I swear that's what I carved on that tombstone. Just R.I.P., and nothing else. But when I went in to work one day, my carving was gone. Somehow the initials C.C. had appeared in its place. And the dates 1882 to 1892."

"What does it mean?" Amy demanded.

"I don't know," Mr. Melman said. "At first I

thought it was just some workman's idea of a sick joke. But as I stood there, I felt the fear coming over me. A terrible, nameless fear! It took all my willpower just to touch the horrible thing. And when I did . . ."

Jessica was sitting on the edge of her seat. "What then?"

Mr. Melman shivered. "When I touched it, I realized that it wasn't my fake wooden tombstone at all. It was cold and hard, like solid granite. Somehow, it had become a *real* tombstone!"

Mr. Melman shook his head. "That was the *last* haunted house I ever designed."

"Wait until you hear about the carnival, Elizabeth!" Jessica rushed into her twin's bedroom as soon as she got home.

Elizabeth was lying on her back on her unmade bed. "Is this about Claire?" she asked eagerly.

"Can't you forget about that girl for one day?" Jessica demanded.

Elizabeth closed her eyes and sighed. "You sound just like Mom and Dad."

"They're just worried about you, Lizzie." Jessica sat on the edge of Elizabeth's bed. "You have to admit that you've been acting awfully weird lately."

"Just because I have a new friend doesn't mean I'm weird!" Elizabeth snapped.

"It's not just that, Elizabeth. You've been having nightmares. You've been really mean to Amy. And just look at your bedroom!" Jessica pointed at the huge mountain of dirty clothes on Elizabeth's floor. "You haven't kept up with your chores at all. It's like you aren't even *you* anymore!" Jessica leaned against Elizabeth's desk and her right hand touched something leathery. "Gross!" she exclaimed, holding up a withered brown banana peel.

"I was hungry," Elizabeth said matter-of-factly.

"About two months ago, from the look of it!" Jessica sat down at Elizabeth's desk. "Elizabeth," she began softly, "I've been talking to Amy, and she's been doing some research on the carnival—"

"I know all about it," Elizabeth interrupted. "Amy thinks there's something fishy about the carnival. She's just jealous of Claire."

"*I* think there's something fishy about the carnival, too," Jessica said quietly.

"Then you're jealous, too!" Elizabeth sat up. Her face was red with anger. "Can't you all just leave me alone?"

"I'm only trying to help—" Jessica began.

"Just get out of my room! Get out!" Elizabeth cried.

Jessica walked to the door, too stunned to

argue. "I was only trying to help," she muttered. Then she closed the door behind her.

"Let me in, quick!"

Jessica pulled open the front door to find a girl wearing a broad-brimmed straw hat over a colorful silk scarf. Her face was barely visible.

"Lila? Is that you under there?" Jessica asked.

"Of course it's me," Lila snapped. "Don't you even recognize your best friend?"

"Not when you're dressed like some weird little old lady." Jessica laughed. "Is that some kind of disguise?"

"Just let me in, Jessica," Lila said quickly. "I don't want to stand out here in the sun all day. You know what the hot sun can do to your hair!"

Jessica led Lila inside. "Aren't you going to take off that silly hat?" she asked.

Lila looked anxiously around the room. Cautiously she undid the string that held her hat in place and pulled the hat off her head. "Is it safe?" she demanded.

"Is *what* safe?" Jessica gave an exasperated sigh. First Elizabeth had started acting strange, and now Lila was beginning. *Is the whole world going crazy?* Jessica thought.

Lila gave Jessica a meaningful look. "Is it safe for me to uncover my hair?"

"Lila!" Jessica exploded. "Is that what this is

all about? I have more important things to worry about!"

"I'm just being careful," Lila explained. "All sorts of things can damage your hair, you know—sunlight, wind, rain, hot, cold, humidity, bats—"

"Bats?" Jessica repeated.

Lila nodded. "I read that they can get tangled in your hair."

"Lila, I can absolutely promise you that we have no bats in our house." Jessica shook her head as Lila carefully untied the scarf. Her shoulder-length brown hair was plastered down as if it were coated with grease. "What have you done?" Jessica blurted.

"It's mousse," Lila explained. "I used the whole can. I figure it will hold my hair in place so it *can't* fall out!"

Jessica snorted. "Lila, I think you're taking this fortune thing way, way too seriously. Your hair is *not* going to fall out!"

"You're taking Mademoiselle Z's curse seriously," Lila pointed out.

"That's different. She's an actual fortune teller," Jessica said hotly. "And at least I don't go around worrying about bats!"

"Hey, girls!" Steven called as he came into the room. "Have you seen Bobo?"

"Bobo? Who's Bobo?" Jessica demanded.

"My pet bat!" Steven said, grinning wickedly.

"He's escaped! The last time he escaped he got tangled in a girl's hair and—"

"Very funny, Steven!" Jessica yelled as her brother dashed from the room. She turned to Lila. "Do you see how silly this all is? Someone slips a prank fortune into the bowl and you end up acting like a crazy person!"

"Prank, huh?" Lila was doubtful. "Who could have played that kind of a prank? You and I wrote all the fortunes, and no one knew where I kept them hidden. *I* certainly didn't write it. Did you?"

"Don't be silly," Jessica said.

"It must have been a supernatural force!" Lila insisted. "What else could have done it?"

"I don't know," Jessica said thoughtfully. "But I'm beginning to get an idea."

"Well, if you figure it out, let me know." Lila reached for her scarf. "But until then, I'm not taking any chances!"

Elizabeth woke up from her nap tangled in her sheets. Her eyes were swollen from crying and her mouth was dry.

She'd been dreaming of Claire, and as she climbed out of bed it seemed as though she could almost hear Claire's sweet voice calling her. *I'm lonely, Elizabeth!* she cried. *Come and play with me now!*

Elizabeth crept halfway down the stairs and

crouched against the railing. The TV was on in the family room, and she could hear Jessica and Steven talking. A moment later she heard a third voice that she recognized as Lila Fowler's.

Elizabeth tiptoed down to the final stair. She peeked cautiously down the hallway toward the kitchen. Her mother was sitting at the table reading the newspaper, her back to Elizabeth.

Elizabeth took a deep, quivery breath. She felt strange sneaking around her family this way, and she had never in her whole life disobeyed her parents. But she didn't have a choice. Claire needed her!

She crept down the hallway past the den, where Jessica and Steven were arguing over what to watch on TV. Slowly Elizabeth opened the front door, hoping it wouldn't creak.

"Elizabeth? Is that you?"

Elizabeth heard Jessica's voice and dashed out into the front yard. In an instant, she was on her bike and pedaling away frantically.

I'm coming, Claire. I'm coming! Elizabeth thought.

Jessica raced out to the front porch just in time to catch a glimpse of Elizabeth disappearing around the corner on her bike. The sky was dark and threatening, and a brisk wind shook the trees.

"Lila!" Jessica called back through the open front door. "I've got to go! I'll call you later!"

"Where are you going?" Lila demanded. "You can't just abandon me!"

Jessica didn't bother to answer. She jumped on her bike and pedaled as fast as she could after Elizabeth. There could be only one place Elizabeth would go, and only one person she would want to see.

What *was* it about Claire that made Elizabeth disobey her parents and sneak out of the house? Of all the strange things Elizabeth had done in the past few days, that was the strangest. Jessica knew that she had to talk some sense into her twin and get her to come home before their parents discovered that Elizabeth was gone.

When the carnival grounds were in view, Jessica slowed down to search the area for any sign of her twin. To her surprise, Elizabeth was already at the gate. Jessica could see that Elizabeth hadn't even bothered to lock her bike to the bike rack. She had simply dropped it by the side of the gravel road.

"Elizabeth!" Jessica called, but her sister was too far away to hear. Jessica began to walk her bike toward the entrance, but the closer she got, the more clearly she remembered Mademoiselle Z's frightening prediction. She could still see the anger in the fortune teller's eyes as she had pronounced her curse: *You will have no future, Jessica Wakefield! No future if you ever return to this carnival!*

Jessica stopped and shivered. Storm clouds

had blotted out the sun, and out over the ocean a jagged flash of lightning pierced the sky. It was only late afternoon, but the black clouds made it seem like night had already fallen.

Suddenly, Jessica spotted a boy racing out of the carnival grounds, shoving people aside in his haste. His face was as white as the T-shirt he was wearing.

As he ran toward Jessica, she recognized him as Patrick Morris, a classmate who was one of the nicest, cutest boys at Sweet Valley Middle School. "Patrick!" she called.

Patrick didn't seem to hear her. He ran right past without even looking at her.

"Patrick!" Jessica shouted again. When he still didn't respond, Jessica dropped her bike, ran after him, and grabbed him by the arm.

Patrick gasped. His face was wild with fear, and it took him a moment to recognize Jessica. "Jessica?" he said at last. "Is it really you?"

"Of course it's me," Jessica said. "What's the matter with you?"

"I . . . I don't know." Patrick shook his head. "Something really strange just happened. Something . . . horrible!"

"Tell me!" Jessica demanded.

"All right." He nodded slowly. "I'll tell you. I just saw a ghost!"

Twelve

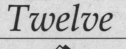

"A ghost?" Jessica exclaimed.

Patrick nodded. "I was on the Ferris wheel and I had a car to myself. The wheel was stopped. You know, so they can let riders get on and off." He shuddered, and Jessica felt her own heart pounding. "Anyway," he continued, "I was at the very top. I was looking out over the ocean when I heard this voice."

"Was it a low, raspy man's voice?" Jessica asked. Could it be the same voice she'd heard at her window?

"No. It was a high voice, like a girl's. It said, 'Hello, Patrick.'" Patrick put his hand over his eyes for a moment before continuing. "I looked around. I figured it was someone in one of the other Ferris-wheel cars, but the ones right below me were empty. I was up there all alone, hundreds of feet in the air. Then I heard the voice again. 'Hello, Patrick,' it said. 'Would you like to come and play?' "

Jessica jumped as a tremendous clap of thunder broke through the air. The storm was coming closer.

"I couldn't see anyone," Patrick went on. "I thought I was going nuts! There was just this voice saying, 'Come and play.' Then I looked harder and I saw something white and kind of wispy. Like a curtain blowing in the breeze."

"That was th-the ghost?" Jessica asked.

"Yes," Patrick said. "It couldn't have been anything else. It was this wispy, white form, standing in mid-air and asking me to come and play. I'll tell you one thing, Jessica. I'm never going on that Ferris wheel again! In fact, I'm going to go home and lock myself in my room until the carnival leaves town for good!" Without another word, Patrick walked quickly away.

Jessica was more than frightened—she was terrified. Mr. Melman's haunting words filled her head. *It felt as if something horrible, something evil had moved in!*

She had to get Elizabeth out! But as she continued toward the carnival gate, Mademoiselle Z's curse rang in her ears. And Jessica was sure that the fortune teller had something to do with whatever evil was stalking the carnival!

"Lizzie!" Jessica cried desperately. "You have to come out!"

Another jagged bolt of lightning raced across the sky, followed by an explosion of thunder. People began to stream out through the clown's-mouth entrance. One by one the rides were being shut down and the bright lights turned off. The sound of the merry-go-round's organ music faded eerily in the wind.

Jessica watched the crowd anxiously, looking for Elizabeth. Out over the ocean rain had already begun to fall, and the storm was moving closer to land. Finally, Jessica spotted her sister wandering through the gate with the last of the crowd.

"Lizzie!" Jessica yelled. "Elizabeth!"

"Jessica!" Elizabeth said in surprise as Jessica ran up to her. "What are you doing here?" She narrowed her eyes. "Did Mom and Dad send you?"

"As a matter of fact, I came here to bring you home before they find out that you're gone," Jessica said.

Heavy drops of rain began to splatter on the ground around them. "They closed the carnival early because of the storm," Elizabeth said unhappily. "I barely got to say hello to Claire."

"I hope the storm washes this horrible carnival into the ocean!" Jessica muttered.

By the time the twins reached home, the rain had stopped, but they were drenched. "Now what do we do?" Jessica wondered aloud as they quietly wheeled their bikes into the garage. "How are we ever going to sneak back into the house without being seen?"

Elizabeth shrugged. "You tell me. You're the one with all the experience."

"Let's see." Jessica wrung out her dripping hair. "It's practically dinnertime, so probably our best bet is to get into the living room through the patio doors. With any luck, Mom and Dad are in the kitchen."

Together the girls sneaked around to the back patio. "The coast is clear!" Jessica whispered as she peeked inside. "Once we're in, run straight upstairs as fast as you can. All right?"

Elizabeth nodded. Jessica eased open one sliding glass door an inch at a time and stepped into the living room. "Come on, Lizzie!" she whispered. "It's safe!"

"Safe from what?"

Jessica gasped and spun around. There, half hidden by the curtains, was Steven, looking very smug.

"Steven!" Jessica hissed. "I thought you were Dad!"

"Sorry to disappoint you," he said. "Looks like you two went for a little dip in the pool. Next time, try swimsuits."

"Steven, you've got to help us!" Jessica pleaded. "Elizabeth's going to be in the worst trouble of her whole life if Mom and Dad find out she sneaked out to the carnival."

Steven looked at Elizabeth and his grin faded. Her face was pale, and there were dark circles under her eyes. "What do you want me to do?" Steven whispered to Jessica.

"Distract Mom and Dad until we can get upstairs and dry off," Jessica whispered back.

"No problem," Steven said confidently. "I'll just ask them for another raise in my allowance. That'll keep them occupied!"

"Thanks!" Jessica said gratefully. She waited until Steven had disappeared from view. Then she grabbed Elizabeth's hand and pulled her upstairs.

The girls quickly changed into dry clothes and dried their hair. Then Jessica decided it was time to tell Elizabeth what had happened to Patrick Morris that afternoon at the carnival.

"Sit down, Elizabeth," she instructed. "I want to make sure you hear all of this."

Elizabeth sat on the edge of the bathtub.

Jessica took a deep breath. "I think that once

you've heard the whole story, it's going to change your mind about the carnival."

"Nothing could do that," Elizabeth said quietly.

"Not even a ghost?" Jessica countered.

"A ghost?" Elizabeth repeated. She stared at Jessica in amazement. "Did you say a *ghost*?"

Jessica nodded. "Patrick Morris saw a ghost while he was on the Ferris wheel."

"Then Patrick's playing a joke on you. Or maybe he's been watching too many scary movies." Elizabeth stood up and smiled. "A ghost! Really, Jessica! You're just jealous of Claire, and you're trying to find some way to scare me away from the carnival."

"I'm not jealous of Claire!" Jessica cried. "I'm worried about the way she's making you sneak around behind Mom and Dad's back!"

"I'll have you know that just this afternoon, Claire told me that I should be nicer to Mom and Dad," Elizabeth said triumphantly.

"She did?" Jessica looked surprised.

"Yes! *Now* what do you think of Claire?" Elizabeth demanded. She turned to leave the bathroom. "I'm going down to set the table."

Jessica shook her head as she watched Elizabeth leave. *I have the feeling that Claire is up to something,* she thought.

Jessica followed her sister downstairs. When

they entered the kitchen, Mr. Wakefield was delivering a lecture to Steven on responsible spending. "As far as I'm concerned, this allowance discussion is closed," Mr. Wakefield said sternly. "Understand, young man?"

"Sorry, Dad," Steven said sheepishly.

Jessica caught her brother's eye and mouthed the word *thanks*.

"So, what have you girls been up to on this rainy day?" Mrs. Wakefield asked as she handed Elizabeth a stack of plates.

"Nothing much," Jessica answered.

"Too bad it had to rain on a vacation day," Mrs. Wakefield said. "By the way, Ned," she said to Mr. Wakefield, "I was just in the living room, and I noticed a big damp spot on the carpet near the sliding doors. You don't think we have a leak in the roof, do you?"

That night, just as Jessica was climbing into bed, the rain began pounding so fiercely against her window that she was afraid the glass would break. Even with her shades drawn, every flash of lightning lit up her entire room and caused eerie shadows to leap across the floor.

Usually Jessica loved storms, but tonight the moaning winds and booming thunder made her very uneasy. "It's just a thunderstorm," she murmured aloud. But every time she closed her eyes, she remembered Patrick Morris's terrifying story. It was obvious that she was going to have a very hard time getting to sleep.

Each time lightning flashed through the sky, Jessica watched the shadow of the big oak tree against her shade. The tree swayed and shivered in the heavy winds, scraping its long branches against the side of the house.

After a while Jessica was almost lulled by the sound. But then something else met her ears. *Tap-tap-tap.* It was the very same terrible noise she'd heard the other night in her nightmare. Only this time, Jessica was absolutely sure she wasn't dreaming!

Jessica dove under her covers. She tried to stay very still, but she couldn't seem to stop trembling.

Tap-tap-tap. The noise came again, louder this time. Could it be the ghost that Patrick had seen, trying to get in out of the storm?

For what seemed like ages, Jessica lay beneath her covers, waiting for the noise to stop. But it only grew louder and more persistent. Beneath her blankets, Jessica felt very hot and stuffy. She knew she would have to get a breath of fresh air soon.

Very slowly she eased down her covers until her mouth and nose were exposed. She took a deep breath of cooler air and felt better. To her relief, the tapping noise seemed to have stopped. Maybe it had just been a branch of the tree after all.

Jessica slowly turned her head toward the window. There was nothing there but her window shade and pretty pink curtains. "I told you so," she murmured to herself.

No sooner had she spoken than a great streak of lightning lit up the room, revealing the terrifying outline of a human skeleton against the window shade. Its bony hand seemed to beckon Jessica from her bed.

Jessica screamed, but her voice was lost in the huge clap of thunder that shook the entire house. A second flash of lightning, even brighter than the first, filled the room, illuminating every corner with blinding white light. Again, the skeleton's shadow flashed on the window shade. Then, in the silence after the thunder's fading rumble, Jessica heard the low, raspy voice. *"Stay away!"*

Jessica closed her eyes and screamed again with all her might. By the time her parents burst into her room, the skeleton had disappeared without a trace.

"Jessica! Jess, wake up!"

Jessica sat up and rubbed her eyes. "Where am I?" she asked groggily.

Elizabeth laughed. "Where do you think,

silly? You're on my bedroom floor!" She sat down next to Jessica on the edge of her sleeping bag. "You had a horrible nightmare last night, remember? You were so upset that you insisted on sleeping in my room."

Jessica's stomach turned a somersault as she remembered the horrifying shadow of the skeleton outside her window. "Elizabeth!" Jessica cried. She grabbed her sister's arm. "It was terrible! There was a skeleton, and every time the lightning flashed I could see it. It was tapping on the window and saying, 'Stay away'!"

Elizabeth patted her sister's back sympathetically. "And you thought *I* was having nightmares! That one really takes the cake."

"But it wasn't a dream, Lizzie!" Jessica protested. "This time I'm *sure* it wasn't!"

Jessica could tell from Elizabeth's smile that she didn't believe her story. "Come on, Jess," Elizabeth said. "Let's go get some breakfast."

In the kitchen, Mrs. Wakefield was preparing pancakes. "Morning, girls!" She gave Jessica an extra-long hug. "How'd you sleep, honey? Your father and I were very worried about you last night."

"I slept fine," Jessica said shortly. There was no point in trying to convince her mother about the skeleton. Her own twin didn't even believe her!

"Mom, let me help you with those pancakes!"
Elizabeth said brightly.

"Why, thank you, Elizabeth." Mrs. Wakefield
winked at Jessica. "Looks like we have our old
Elizabeth back!"

"I want to apologize for the way I've been
acting lately," Elizabeth said sweetly. She carried
a plate of pancakes over to Jessica. "I think you
were right, Mom. I *did* have a touch of the flu,
after all. But after resting all day yesterday, I feel
much better!"

Jessica stared at her twin. *Resting?* she
thought.

Mrs. Wakefield seemed very relieved. "You've
had us all worried about you, Elizabeth," she said.
"I can't tell you how glad I am to see you smiling
again."

Elizabeth placed a bottle of maple syrup on
the kitchen table. "You know, Claire called yesterday," she continued, avoiding Jessica's gaze. "It
seems she had the flu, too. I guess it's going
around."

"That's too bad," Mrs. Wakefield said.

"Anyway, she wanted me to apologize for
her. She felt just awful about missing dinner on
New Year's Day."

"Why didn't she call?" Jessica asked pointedly.

"She was too sick. In fact, her whole family
was sick." Elizabeth smiled at Mrs. Wakefield.

"You know, Mom, the carnival will be leaving in a day. I was wondering if I could have permission to visit the carnival this afternoon. I'd like to invite Claire and her family for lunch tomorrow, before they leave town."

"Can I count on you to come home on time?" Mrs. Wakefield asked.

"Of course," Elizabeth assured her.

"Well, I suppose it would be all right," Mrs. Wakefield said. "Your father and I are going to a barbecue this evening. We'll be leaving this afternoon, so I need to know that I can trust you both to behave. That means I want you home no later than five o'clock, Elizabeth."

"Thanks, Mom!" Elizabeth gave her mother a kiss on the cheek.

"Don't you think Elizabeth should stay home until she's fully recovered?" Jessica looked hard at her mother.

"She seems fine to me," Mrs. Wakefield answered. Elizabeth flashed her mother a dazzling smile.

"Not to me," Jessica murmured, but no one seemed to notice.

In spite of her initial doubts, as the day wore on Jessica had to admit that Elizabeth did seem like her old self again. She cleaned up her room, dusted the furniture in the living room, and helped Jessica to fold the clean clothes from the laundry. She joked with and teased Jessica and Steven, and even called Amy and promised to meet her the next morning for a bike ride.

"Are you sure I finally have the *real* Elizabeth back?" Jessica asked when Elizabeth had finished talking to Amy.

"Positive!" Elizabeth laughed.

"Good, because I was getting awfully tired of being the responsible twin! Which reminds me—" Jessica lowered her voice. "Are you in the mood for a little spy activity?"

"Sounds interesting. Whom are we spying on?"

"Our big brother." Jessica led Elizabeth to the doorway of Steven's bedroom. "Trust me. He has it coming. I have a sneaking suspicion that he played a very mean trick on Lila and me."

The twins peered into Steven's bedroom. It was far messier than Jessica's bedroom was at its very worst. "He's outside playing basketball, so I know it's safe," Jessica whispered.

"Are you sure we should be sneaking in here?" Elizabeth asked nervously. "It doesn't seem right."

"Lizzie!" Jessica laughed affectionately. "Now I *know* you're back to normal!" She tiptoed over to Steven's desk. "I'm just trying to prove my theory. You remember Lila's fortune?"

"I heard you two talking about it," Elizabeth nodded. "Something about going bald?"

Jessica nodded. "Well, I think Steven wrote it. He must have sneaked it into our pile of fortunes the day Lila and I wrote them. But to prove it, I have to find a sample of Steven's handwriting."

"How about this?" Elizabeth asked. She pulled a crumpled piece of paper out of Steven's wastebasket. "It's an old quiz from his French class."

"Let me see!" Jessica examined the paper. "Hmm," she said. "An A minus. Not bad!" She reached into the pocket of her jeans and pulled out a little slip of paper. "This is Lila's fortune," Jessica said. "I saved it for evidence." She held the little slip next to a row of answers on Steven's quiz. "Just as I thought!" she cried. "This *is* his handwriting! I was almost certain it was Steven's, but I had to have proof."

"Now what, Inspector?" Elizabeth asked.

Jessica tossed Steven's quiz back in the wastebasket. "Now we plot our revenge!" she exclaimed.

The girls wandered into Elizabeth's bedroom. "While you decide Steven's fate, I'm going to ride on over to the carnival," Elizabeth said. She reached for her backpack, but Jessica snatched it away.

"No, Lizzie!" she cried. "*Please* don't go!"

"Jess, don't be silly!" Elizabeth said impatiently. "Mom said it was OK. And I promised her I'll be back by five."

"But what about Patrick Morris?" Jessica persisted. "Have you forgotten about what happened to him?"

Elizabeth smiled. "No, I haven't forgotten. And I promise I won't talk to any ghosts while I'm there. Now are you satisfied?"

"Please, Lizzie," Jessica pleaded. "There's something horrible going on at that carnival. I don't know what it is, but I know it's not safe!"

"Will you let go of my backpack, Jessica?" Elizabeth was still smiling, but her voice was strained.

Reluctantly Jessica released Elizabeth's backpack. "Why won't you listen to me?" she asked softly.

"I listen to you, Jessica." Elizabeth laughed. "I just don't believe you!"

Thirteen

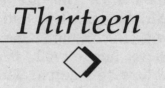

"Mom and Dad left *me* in charge, and *I* decide what we watch!" Steven declared. He clicked the remote control buttons until a car chase appeared on the TV screen.

"They may have left you in charge," Jessica replied, "but no one made you dictator!"

"Well, you owe me," Steven said. "You and Elizabeth would have been grounded for life if Mom and Dad had caught you sneaking in yesterday." He glanced at his watch. "Where is Elizabeth, anyway? Wasn't she supposed to be home by now?"

Jessica nodded. "She's practically two hours late. I *knew* I shouldn't have let her go to that carnival today."

"What's the big deal? I thought that curse was only on you," Steven teased.

"It's dangerous there, Steven," Jessica said. "You just don't understand."

He laughed. "You're right about that!"

For a moment, Jessica considered telling her brother about Patrick Morris's experience and about what Mr. Melman had told her and Amy. But what was the point? She knew Steven wouldn't believe her. "Well, if Elizabeth isn't home by the time this stupid TV show is over, then I'm really going to . . ."

"Going to *what*?" Steven wanted to know.

"Going to be worried," Jessica said softly. What could she do? She couldn't exactly go to the carnival herself—not with Mademoiselle Z's curse still hanging over her head! And what about the horrible voice that had warned her to stay away? Just being *near* the carnival the day before had scared her half to death!

"Elizabeth probably just forgot about the time," Steven said. "Stop worrying, shrimp."

But when another hour had passed without Elizabeth's coming home, Jessica became frantic. She began to pace up and down, and to check the window every few minutes for signs of her sister.

"Stop pacing, will you?" Steven demanded. "I'm getting seasick just watching you!"

"It's dark out, and it's starting to get really

foggy," Jessica said. "Elizabeth has never stayed out this late before."

"I'm sure she's fine," Steven said, suddenly not sounding sure at all.

As Jessica continued to stare out of the window, the telephone rang. "Elizabeth!" she cried. "That's her! I just know it!" She dashed to the telephone in the kitchen. "Hello?" she answered breathlessly.

"The girl is in danger!" said a low, raspy man's voice. "Terrible danger!"

"Who—who is this?" Jessica managed to ask. The lump in her throat was so big that she could barely speak.

"Get her away from here, or you will never see her again on this side of the grave!" the voice said urgently. "Quickly! The evil one is ready to strike!"

"Who—" Jessica began, but the line had already gone dead.

"Lizzie!" Jessica cried. There was no doubt about it. Elizabeth was in danger! And Jessica had to do something to save her! But what? If *she* went to the carnival, she might be in just as much danger. She could try to convince Steven to help, but he still wasn't likely to believe her. And she would waste valuable time trying to convince him.

"Amy!" Jessica snatched up the phone. With trembling fingers she dialed Amy's number. *Amy will believe me*, Jessica thought. *Amy will want to help Elizabeth!*

But Amy's phone rang and rang, and no one answered. At last Jessica gave up and tried Lila's number. "Lila, I need your help!" Jessica cried when her friend answered the phone.

"I just conditioned my hair," Lila said. "Can't it wait?"

"No, it *can't* wait!" Jessica snapped. "Elizabeth is in terrible danger, and someone has to get her out of the carnival as soon as possible!"

"The carnival?" Lila repeated. "Are you kidding? You know I won't go near that place!"

"But Lila," Jessica said frantically "this is a matter of life and—"

"And besides," Lila continued, "I have to leave this conditioner on my hair for thirty minutes. It's supposed to give it extra body and—"

"Just forget it, Lila!" Jessica slammed down the receiver.

She was wasting precious time. She could call her parents, but it would take them at least an hour to drive home. *Quickly!* the man had said. *The evil one is ready to strike!*

There was no other way. Only one person could save Elizabeth. No matter what the danger, Jessica would have to defy Mademoiselle Z and rescue Elizabeth!

*　　*　　*

Jessica's hands trembled as she locked her bike to the bicycle rack outside the carnival entrance. The carnival grounds were even more frightening late at night. A thick fog was moving in from the sea, and had already hidden the moon. The huge Ferris wheel was just a dim blur of colored lights.

She paused before the clown's-mouth entrance. Somehow, it no longer seemed funny. To Jessica, it looked like the macabre grin of a rotting skull, or the hungry mouth of some awful beast, ready to swallow her up.

"Are you coming, or what?" the gate attendant demanded.

"Um . . . yes. I'm coming in," Jessica answered in a shaky voice.

"Well, hurry up!" the attendant growled. "We close in twenty minutes. Maybe sooner, if this fog gets any thicker."

"Yes, I know." Jessica nodded. For a brief moment she considered waiting outside the gate until closing time. Elizabeth was sure to come out then. And Jessica would be safe from Mademoiselle Z's curse.

She started to turn away. But then Jessica recalled the words of the man on the phone. *Quickly!* he had warned.

Jessica couldn't take the chance of waiting.

Elizabeth needed her help, and she needed it right now.

As she stepped through the clown's gaping mouth, Jessica's knees felt like rubber. *Now I've disobeyed Mademoiselle Z*, she thought fearfully. *What will happen to me?* Jessica took another step. The fog wrapped itself around her like a smothering shroud.

Jessica had no idea where to find Elizabeth. Even though it was near closing time, there was still a bustling crowd of people.

Jessica began by searching along the rows of food booths, most of which were being shut up for the night. Elizabeth was nowhere to be seen.

Jessica ran on to the game booths. By the time she reached the shooting gallery, she felt as if her lungs would burst. Beads of nervous sweat were rolling down her cheeks, and her clothes clung to her body.

She raced on again through the crowd of people, who were scurrying around like gray phantoms. She stopped to catch her breath beside the Tilt-a-Whirl and tried to peer into each spinning car as it slowed to a stop. When she was positive that Elizabeth wasn't in any of the cars, she staggered on to the roller coaster.

One by one, the rides were being turned off all around her. The organ music from the merry-go-round ground to a halt, and the lights strung overhead from booth to booth blinked on and off to signal the carnival's close.

Jessica peered frantically at the faces streaming past her. What if it was already too late? "Elizabeth!" she yelled. "Lizzie!"

"You lost, young lady?"

Jessica spun around to find a carnival employee, a young man with a scraggly brown mustache, standing behind her.

"I'm looking for my sister," Jessica said.

"What does she look like?" the man asked.

"Well, she's blond, and has blue-green eyes, and—" Jessica slapped her forehead. "How stupid! She looks like me! We're identical twins!"

"Hmm." The man stroked his chin. "I saw someone who looked like you a while back. But then again, it could have been you."

"She was dressed differently," Jessica said. "She was wearing—"

The man shook his head. "I don't notice what folks are wearing."

"I know!" Jessica said suddenly. "She would probably have been with Claire!"

The man looked puzzled. "Who?"

"Claire! The carnival owners' daughter, Claire," Jessica said.

"The owner's daughter?" the man echoed. "This carnival's owned by the Austin Entertainment Corporation. Maybe you mean the manager, although I'm pretty sure that old Mr. Mates doesn't have a daughter. I don't believe he's ever been married. Of course, I could be wrong. I've only been with the carnival about a year." He snapped his fingers. "I'll tell you who *would* know, though: Mrs. Zalekis. She's been with the carnival her whole life."

"Mrs. Za—what?" Jessica asked.

"She calls herself Mademoiselle Z," the man said. "The Z is short for Zalekis."

"Oh, no!" Jessica moaned.

The man pointed. "Her tent is over by—"

"Thank you," Jessica interrupted. "I know where her tent is." *And it's the last place I want to go,* she thought grimly.

But Jessica realized that she had already searched the entire carnival except for two places: the haunted house and Mademoiselle Z's tent. And while she did not want to go to either place, she knew that she had to find her sister.

Well, I might as well get it over with, Jessica told herself. *I'll search the haunted house first.*

Though the attendant had gone, the haunted house had been left unlocked. "Elizabeth, if you're in there, you'd better come out this minute!" Jessica yelled.

She waited, hoping desperately that Elizabeth would answer, but the only sound she could hear was the wind whistling through the ramshackle building. Slowly Jessica stepped inside.

The door creaked shut behind her. All of the scary red and blue lights had been turned off. The only illumination came from a few dim safety lights at the far corners.

The skeletons no longer glowed. They just looked dusty, and it was easy to see that they were made of plastic. The cackling witch was silent, and Jessica could tell that her gleaming red eyes were really Christmas-tree bulbs. The ax blade hung limply in the air.

But somehow, with the phony equipment dull and silent, the haunted house was more frightening than ever. Jessica was no longer concerned with mechanically produced loud noises and eerie lights. Her fear was far more real. She was all alone in this strange place, and no one in the world knew where she was!

"Elizabeth, I can't believe you're making me go through all this!" Jessica whispered.

Jessica walked on toward the doors marked Vampires and Ghosts. "Which should I choose?" Jessica murmured.

"Ghosts, of course," a voice said.

Jessica screamed and turned around. Her eyes searched the room frantically but she could see no one and nothing.

"I'm hearing things!" Jessica said aloud, in an

attempt at bravery. "I'm so scared that I'm starting to imagine things." Still, one thing was certain. She was definitely *not* about to go through the door marked Ghosts.

Jessica walked over to the door marked VAMPIRES and pulled on the handle. It would not budge.

"No, no!" Jessica cried. Quickly she retraced her steps through the haunted house. When she reached the entrance, she pushed hard on the door. Then she pulled.

The door was locked! And now the only possible way out of the haunted house was through the door marked GHOSTS!

Something evil had moved in there! Mr. Melman's words thundered in her ears. Tears filled Jessica's eyes as she walked slowly back toward the awful door. "I really don't want to do this!" she moaned. "Elizabeth, I am *never* going to forgive you for getting me into this mess!"

Jessica's heart was pounding wildly as she opened the door and stepped through it. On either side of the pathway, white sheets with empty eyes hung lifelessly. Jessica tiptoed past them. *What's so scary about a bunch of dirty old sheets?* she asked herself. But her teeth were chattering and her knees felt wobbly. Then she saw the open grave—and the tombstone that Mr. Melman said had somehow become real.

Jessica heard a rustling behind her. She turned around very slowly.

One of the sheets was floating in mid-air! And through the eye holes Jessica could see two dark, solemn eyes staring directly into her own.

Jessica cried out in terror, turned, and raced down the pathway into the open grave. She threw open the door at the end of the path and found herself face-to-face with the headless ghoul.

Jessica screamed again and crashed against the exit door.

The door was locked.

Again, she slammed into it, but still it would not give. Finally, with her last ounce of strength, Jessica backed up and ran at the door. And then she slammed against something soft.

Jessica looked up into the face of Mademoiselle Z's huge assistant. Fog swirled around him, billowing in through the open door.

"Don't be afraid," the man said in a low, raspy voice.

It was the very same voice that Jessica had heard at her bedroom window! She moaned and turned to dart away.

But it's also the voice that called today to warn me about Elizabeth. Jessica remembered. She stopped in her tracks. *Does he know where Elizabeth is?*

"Don't be afraid," the man repeated. "We are your friends."

"We?" Jessica repeated.

"You must come with me to see Mademoiselle Z," he said. "She wants only to help you."

Something in his tone of voice made Jessica believe him. And at least he and Mademoiselle Z were *real*!

"Follow me," the man said as he led Jessica through the dense fog and toward the fortune teller's blue tent. For a moment, Jessica felt hopeful.

But when they arrived at the tent a few moments later, Jessica couldn't quite bring herself to step inside.

"Go on," the man urged. "She will not harm you."

Jessica took one step forward.

"There you are!" Mademoiselle Z cried. "You're all right!" She pulled Jessica quickly inside. "Thank goodness we got to you in time!"

"In time for what?" Jessica asked.

"In time to save your life, you silly girl!" Her eyes flashed with anger. "Why did you come back here? I told you to stay away if you valued your life!"

"If you were trying to save me, why did you put that awful curse on me?" Jessica demanded.

"I put the curse on you to keep you away from the carnival," Mademoiselle Z explained. "I could see that you were in terrible danger, so I tried to scare you away. But when you came back, I had to try even harder to frighten you."

Jessica shook her head in confusion. "What do you mean?"

"I sent my fiancé, Nicolai, to scare you." She pointed at the bald man who had followed Jessica inside.

Jessica's head was spinning. *"He's* your fiancé?"

"Yes." Mademoiselle Z nodded. "I remembered your name—Jessica Wakefield. We found your address in the telephone book. Nicolai waited outside your house until he saw you looking out of your bedroom window. Then we made our plan."

"It was your fiancé who tapped on my window in the middle of the night!" Jessica cried. "So it wasn't a dream after all!"

"No, it was no dream," Mademoiselle Z said. "Nicolai could reach your window from the big tree in the yard. He was responsible for the tapping noises, the whispered warnings, and finally the plastic skeleton."

"But why?" Jessica asked. "Why did you want me to stay away from the carnival?"

"Let me tell you a story." Mademoiselle Z sat down in her chair, behind the big crystal ball. "Many years ago a man and his wife were trapeze artists in the circus. One night during a performance the man was injured very badly. Because he could no longer work for the circus, he formed this traveling carnival. He and his wife had a child, but they were never a happy family. The father was bitter about the accident, and he was cruel to his wife and daughter."

Mademoiselle Z took a deep breath. "When the little girl was still very young, her mother died after a long illness. Her father grew even more unhappy, and he inflicted his anguish on the little girl. She was not allowed to have any playmates, and he forbade her to go on any of the rides. Over time, the little girl grew as cruel and bitter as her father.

"On her tenth birthday, the girl asked her father for a special gift. For one night she wanted to be like any other normal child and to go on the rides.

"But her father refused. That night the little girl decided to go on the Ferris wheel all by herself. After everyone had gone to sleep, she sneaked outside and managed to start the huge wheel and hop into a car."

"What happened to her?" Jessica asked nervously.

"She rode for hours until at last she grew tired," Mademoiselle Z answered. "As her car reached the ground, she jumped off. But her long dress got caught in the car and she couldn't pull it free. The wheel continued to turn, and the poor little girl was pulled to the very top of the Ferris wheel. She hung there for just a moment, hundreds of feet in the air, until her dress finally tore."

Mademoiselle Z shook her head sadly. "They found the little girl's body on the ground the next morning. The Ferris wheel was still turning. Caught on one of the cars was a long strip of blue-and-cream fabric, floating in the breeze. Her father sold the carnival the very next day."

"What a terrible story!" Jessica exclaimed. "But what does it have to do with me?"

"Can't you guess?" Mademoiselle Z asked. "Don't you understand? The little girl died, but her unhappy spirit didn't go away. Soon afterward, children who visited the carnival began to report strange sights and sounds. Some people believed that she inhabited the haunted house.

"I was one of those children who saw her. I, too, was raised in the carnival. My mother was the fortune teller before me. And when I was about your age, the girl's ghost first came to me and asked me to play." Mademoiselle Z looked away. "I remember it as if it were yesterday, though it has been more than thirty years. She was a solemn little girl with jet black hair. She said her name was—"

"Claire!" Jessica cried.

Fourteen

"Yes." Mademoiselle Z nodded her head solemnly. "The little girl you have been playing with has been dead for nearly a century."

"Oh, no!" Jessica jumped to her feet.

"That's why I tried to scare you away, but you kept coming back. You should have listened to me!" Mademoiselle Z exclaimed.

"But I *did*, Mademoiselle Z!" Jessica said. "This is the first time I've been back to the carnival since you cursed me."

"That's impossible," Mademoiselle Z said firmly. "I saw you several times with Claire!"

Jessica shook her head. "No, Mademoiselle Z. You saw Elizabeth, my twin sister!"

Mademoiselle Z's eyes widened with disbelief. "Your—your twin sister? Then—"

"It was Elizabeth who was playing with Claire!" Jessica cried.

Mademoiselle Z grabbed Jessica's arm. "Has she seemed strange to you lately? Distracted or forgetful?"

"Yes! It's as if she isn't even herself anymore. The only person she spends time with is Claire," Jessica said. "And—and she's been having nightmares and talking in her sleep."

Mademoiselle Z frowned. "She has fallen under Claire's power. Claire can only be seen by her intended victims, and over time she draws them further and further into her world. She makes them forget their friends and their family. She can even control their thoughts—only a little at first, but then more and more, until they are completely under her spell!"

"We have to find Elizabeth!" Jessica cried.

"Yes!" Mademoiselle Z agreed, "and there isn't a minute to lose!"

"Where is she?" Jessica asked desperately.

"Don't *you* know?" Mademoiselle Z asked.

"No! Can't you use your mystical powers to find her?" Jessica asked.

"Mystical powers?" Mademoiselle Z laughed bitterly. "I have no powers. What your friend said is true. I'm a fake."

"But you said you could see Claire, even though she's invisible!" Jessica persisted.

"Yes, I can see Claire," Mademoiselle Z said. "Because I was almost her victim and because she chose to show herself to me. But I cannot fight her. She's much too powerful!"

"What can we do?" Jessica demanded.

Mademoiselle Z hesitated a moment. Then she turned to her husband. "Nicolai! Let the ponies out of the stable. Let them run freely through the carnival!"

Nicolai nodded and ducked out of the tent.

"The ponies—all animals, in fact—are terrified of ghosts. They sense their presence and are afraid!" Mademoiselle Z explained. "We'll know by their screams that Claire is nearby."

"That day when you said bad things would happen to my friend Lila—" Jessica wondered.

"Yes, I was angry. I'm sorry," Mademoiselle Z said.

"But when Lila left your tent, one of the ponies suddenly panicked and frightened her!" Jessica remembered.

"Was your sister nearby?" Mademoiselle Z asked.

Jessica tried hard to remember. "Yes. Yes, she was only a few feet away."

"Then Claire must have been there, too!" Mademoiselle Z said.

Jessica shivered. She had been just a few feet

away from a terrible, evil ghost! *But Elizabeth is even closer,* she realized. *She's with Claire now!*

Just then they heard the terrified whinny of a pony far off in the distance.

Elizabeth felt as if she were trapped in a bad dream. She and Claire had spent the afternoon together, wandering the carnival grounds as they always did. But when night had fallen, her friend had suddenly changed. Claire had become bossy and mean.

At first Elizabeth had been annoyed, but when Claire looked directly into her eyes, Elizabeth's annoyance disappeared. A sort of apathy had settled in its place.

"The carnival is leaving Sweet Valley tomorrow, Elizabeth," Claire said as they walked across the empty carnival grounds. It was after closing, and all the colored lights were off. Dense fog hung thickly around them.

"Yes," Elizabeth said dully.

"But we will still be able to play together."

Elizabeth shook her head in confusion. "How?"

"You'll be going with me, of course," Claire said. "You're far too good a friend for me ever to let you go. What would I do without you? I'd be so lonely."

"But how can I go with you?" Elizabeth asked dreamily. "My family, my friends . . ."

"I'll take care of everything, Elizabeth," Claire assured her. "You just do what I say. You *will* do whatever I say, won't you, Elizabeth?"

For a moment Elizabeth had the urge to argue with Claire, but when she tried to say no, she was overcome with dizziness. "Yes," she said at last.

"Yes *what*, Elizabeth?" Claire prompted.

"Yes, I'll do whatever you say, Claire," Elizabeth answered meekly.

"Good." Claire sounded satisfied. "Shall we go on a ride?"

"But . . . but you never want to go on the rides," Elizabeth said.

"I want *you* to go on a ride, Elizabeth. I want you to go on the Ferris wheel," Claire insisted.

"The Ferris wheel?" Elizabeth asked.

"It's my favorite ride." Claire's dark eyes glittered. "I went on it once, a long, long time ago."

Elizabeth looked around her dully.

"Hurry up, Elizabeth," Claire demanded. "Bad people are coming to try and stop us."

Elizabeth could barely make out the Ferris wheel ahead. Its lights were off and it was still. "The carnival is closed," Elizabeth said flatly.

"Climb the steps to the Ferris wheel and get into that first car," Claire ordered.

"But it's closed," Elizabeth tried to argue.

"You promised to do as I say, Elizabeth. *Now do it!*" Claire commanded.

Slowly Elizabeth climbed up to the Ferris wheel and sat down in the first car. Something struggled to the surface of Elizabeth's mind as she sat patiently in the car. A memory from what seemed like a long time ago. A memory of a tiny piece of paper and . . . a *message*.

The Ferris wheel's lights flickered on and the motor suddenly began to whir.

Then there was another sound—the sound of a pony whinnying loudly. Elizabeth looked down to see Jasper rearing in panic.

Claire held herself perfectly still. Then she opened her mouth and released a terrifying growl. Jasper screamed and galloped off.

With a lurch, the Ferris wheel began to turn.

Jessica and Mademoiselle Z raced from the tent toward the sound of the frightened horse. The animal's cries seemed to be coming from the area near the Ferris wheel.

"Be careful of Claire," Mademoiselle Z warned as she hurried alongside Jessica. "If Claire makes herself visible to you, don't be fooled by her innocent appearance. Claire is an evil spirit, very powerful and very dangerous. You cannot fight her!"

"Then how can we save Elizabeth?" Jessica cried.

"Only Elizabeth can stop Claire now," Mademoiselle Z said. "Claire has spent far more time with Elizabeth than she has ever spent with an intended victim. And her control of Elizabeth is great! Your sister will have to be very strong to resist."

"What is Claire going to do to Elizabeth?" Jessica demanded. "Tell me!"

"She will ask Elizabeth to join her," Mademoiselle Z said. "But in the end, Elizabeth will have to decide."

"To decide?" Jessica repeated.

Mademoiselle Z said quietly, "To decide whether she will stay with the living—or join Claire."

"Look!" Jessica cried. "The Ferris wheel's lights are on!"

Suddenly, Jasper raced past them.

"There she is!" Jessica could see Elizabeth all alone in a car of the Ferris wheel. *And the wheel was beginning to move!*

"Nicolai!" Mademoiselle Z screamed. She and Jessica watched as Nicolai raced up to the Ferris-wheel platform and threw his shoulder against the long control lever. The Ferris wheel lurched to a stop. Elizabeth's car was only a few feet in the air.

"Hold on, Elizabeth! I'm coming!" Jessica dashed up the steps of the platform and grabbed hold of the bottom of Elizabeth's car. As she began to pull herself up into the car, Jessica heard a deafening roar. She looked behind her and for the first time she saw Claire, standing face-to-face with Nicolai.

Claire howled with laughter. "Out of my way!" she roared. Slowly her dark eyes rolled back in her head. The empty sockets glowed like fire. Nicolai fell backward, clutching his chest.

"Claire!" Mademoiselle screamed. "Let the girl go! You can take me—but let her go!"

"How nice of you to offer." Claire laughed wildly. "But what would I do with you? You had your chance fifteen years ago. You could have been my friend forever!"

"I—I've changed my mind," Mademoiselle Z cried frantically. "I want to be your friend. Only let the girl go free!"

"No! And now it looks as if I may have *two* playmates!" Slowly Claire stretched out her hand and pulled the Ferris-wheel control lever toward her.

Jessica had struggled halfway into Elizabeth's car when the wheel lurched to a start. The ground fell away quickly, but with her last bit of strength, Jessica pulled herself completely into the car.

"Lizzie!" she cried. "Lizzie, talk to me!"

But Elizabeth stared straight ahead, as if she did not even see her sister.

Jessica grabbed her arm. "Lizzie! It's me, Jessica!"

Elizabeth's eyes flickered, but she continued to stare blankly ahead.

The Ferris wheel was still turning. Jessica felt dizzy as she looked out over the carnival. Already they were as high as a five-story building.

Suddenly the Ferris wheel jerked to a stop. Jessica and Elizabeth were at the very top of the wheel. Below them, the carnival grounds were nearly invisible in the fog. But off in the distance the fog had cleared, and Jessica could see the lights of their own neighborhood.

"Elizabeth! Look!" Jessica put her hands on Elizabeth's shoulders and forced her to turn her head. "Can't you see, Elizabeth? Our home is just over there! Mom and Dad and Steven. They all want you to come home!"

Jessica glanced down again at the ground and groaned. Claire had begun to float upward, as easily as if she were being hoisted on invisible strings!

Slowly she rose until she was floating in the air only a few feet in front of the twins' car. "Come, Elizabeth," Claire said. "Come to me. It's time to play!"

Fifteen

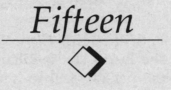

Elizabeth saw Claire floating before her, smiling and calling to her. Claire wanted her to come and play!

Slowly Elizabeth began to stand up. But something seemed to be holding her in place. Elizabeth glanced down in confusion.

For the first time, Elizabeth realized that there was another person in the car with her, and that she had her arms wrapped around Elizabeth's waist. The person seemed familiar in some way, and she was saying something. But Elizabeth couldn't place the person, and she couldn't understand her words.

"Come, Elizabeth!" Claire called. "Come to me."

Again Elizabeth struggled to stand. But the other person in the car refused to let her go.

"Look at me, Elizabeth," Claire commanded. "Look into my eyes."

Elizabeth gazed out at Claire.

"I'm your friend, Elizabeth." Claire's voice was harsh and angry. "I'm your best friend in the whole world."

Yes, Elizabeth thought. *Claire is my very best friend.* Again she heard the familiar voice. It was coming from the person next to her.

"No, Elizabeth!" Jessica cried. "I'm your sister, and we will always be the best friends in the whole world."

"Jessica?" Elizabeth said uncertainly.

"Enough!" Claire growled. "Come to me *now*!"

Elizabeth stood up abruptly, pulling free of Jessica's grasp.

"Come to me!" Claire commanded. "Come to me!"

"No, Elizabeth!" Jessica screamed.

Elizabeth put one leg over the rail. Jessica grabbed hold of Elizabeth's waist again and held on with all of her might.

"You promised to do as I said!" Claire cried.

Jessica watched in horror as Claire began to transform before them. Her long black hair turned white and scraggly. Her girlish face grew sunken and bony, and her flesh dried and withered. Finally, nothing was left of Claire but a hideous skeleton.

"Look at her, Elizabeth!" Jessica screamed. "She's not a girl! She's an evil, horrible ghost!"

"Come to me, Elizabeth!" Claire croaked.

Elizabeth leaned forward, stretching out her arms to the beckoning skeleton.

"No, Elizabeth!" Jessica commanded. "You *can't* go! I need you!"

Suddenly a dazzling light exploded from the skeleton's eye sockets, and Elizabeth felt it strike very near her. She looked down and saw Jessica, her own sister, in the bottom of the car. She was clutching her arm and crying.

Elizabeth struggled to understand what was happening. *My sister is hurt*, she told herself. *And Claire is the one who hurt her!*

"Come to me, Elizabeth!" Claire called.

Claire hurt Jessica! Elizabeth realized.

"I order you to come to me now!" Claire shrieked.

"No! No, Claire, I will not!" Elizabeth yelled.

With a scream that seemed to rattle the air around her, Claire writhed and twisted in fury. Suddenly Elizabeth could see the true Claire—the bitter, long-dead, monstrous spirit who had hoped to make Elizabeth become like her.

As the twins watched, Claire let out one last

agonized scream. What was left of her slowly faded into the foggy night, and she was gone.

Elizabeth sank back into the car and helped Jessica onto the seat. She gave her sister a long, tight hug. "Are you OK?" she whispered.

Jessica rubbed her arm, and her eyes filled again with tears. "I'm fine," she sobbed. "But you sure owe me for this one, Lizzie!"

Elizabeth walked into the living room just as Jessica was finishing a phone conversation with Lila.

"OK, Lila. See you soon," Jessica said, smiling broadly as she hung up the receiver.

"Did you tell her what happened last night?" Elizabeth asked.

Jessica looked at her twin. "Lila? Are you kidding? She'd never believe me in a million years. Are you going to tell Amy?"

Elizabeth sat down next to Jessica on the couch. "I guess I'll try," she said. "But the time I spent with Claire is like a bad dream. I can't seem to remember much at all."

"That's probably just as well." Jessica nodded. "Should we tell Mom and Dad?"

"Do you think they would believe us?" Elizabeth asked.

Jessica shook her head. "How about Steven?"

Elizabeth giggled. "I *know* he wouldn't believe us!"

"I'm sure glad we got home before Mom and Dad last night, or we would have had a lot of explaining to do!" Jessica said. "Did Mom ask you anything about Claire?"

"Well, she wanted to know if Claire would be stopping by for lunch before the carnival left today," Elizabeth said. "I told her that Claire had an unexpected appointment she had to keep."

"Hey, Jessica!" Steven called.

"I'm in the living room!" Jessica said.

Steven entered carrying a long envelope. "I guess this is for you," he said as he tossed it to Jessica.

" 'The Amazing Mademoiselle J,' " Jessica murmured, reading the beautiful, feminine handwriting.

Jessica tore open the envelope and pulled out a piece of cream-colored stationery. Printed in gold letters across the top was the name *Irene Zalekis.*

"It's from Mademoiselle Z!" Jessica exclaimed. She read the note aloud.

Dear Jessica,

Although I have no mystical powers, I would like to offer you one final prediction: you and your sister will always

share a special bond of love and friend-
ship. Treasure it and protect it, for you
are truly lucky.

This comes from my heart, not from
my crystal ball, and so I know it must be
true.

Mademoiselle Z

Jessica put down the letter and shook her
head. "What an amazing lady," she said.

Just then the doorbell rang. Elizabeth jumped
up to answer it, but Jessica grabbed her arm.
"Why don't we let Steven get the door?" she said
with a sly grin. "He could use the exercise."

The doorbell rang again, and Steven stomped
down the hallway past the living room. "All right,
already!" he grumbled. "I'm coming!"

The twins listened as he swung open the
door. "Hi, Steven!" came Lila's voice.

Suddenly, Steven screamed. A moment later,
the twins heard his bedroom door slam shut.

"What in the world is wrong with him?" Elizabeth asked.

"It's not what's wrong with Steven." Jessica
winked. "It's what's wrong with Lila." She nodded toward the hallway. "Come on."

Elizabeth followed Jessica to the doorway.
Lila stood on the front porch with a huge grin on
her face.

And no hair on her head.

"Nice bald wig," Jessica commented. "It's very becoming."

"Thanks," Lila said as she stepped inside. "I got it at the same costume shop where I got my witch outfit." She peered up the stairway. "I have a funny feeling that Steven doesn't like my new look."

"Give him a chance," Elizabeth said. "Maybe it'll grow on him!"

The three girls laughed. "See, Lizzie?" Jessica said. "We don't need any visiting carnivals. We have our own right here at home!"

**Join Jessica and Elizabeth for
big adventure in exciting
SWEET VALLEY TWINS SUPER EDITIONS
and SWEET VALLEY TWINS CHILLERS.**

☐ **#1: CLASS TRIP**   15588-1/$3.50
☐ **#2: HOLIDAY MISCHIEF**   15641-1/$3.50
☐ **#3: THE BIG CAMP SECRET**   15707-8/$3.50
☐ **#4: THE UNICORNS GO HAWAIIAN**   15948-8/$3.50

☐ **SWEET VALLEY TWINS SUPER SUMMER
FUN BOOK by Laurie Pascal Wenk**   15816-3/$3.50

Elizabeth shares her favorite summer projects &
Jessica gives you pointers on parties. Plus:
fashion tips, space to record your favorite
summer activities, quizzes, puzzles, a summer
calendar, photo album, scrapbook, address book
& more!

CHILLERS

☐ **#1: THE CHRISTMAS GHOST**   15767-1/$3.50
☐ **#2: THE GHOST IN THE GRAVEYARD**
                                              15801-5/$3.50
☐ **#3: THE CARNIVAL GHOST**   15859-7/$3.50
☐ **#4: THE GHOST IN THE BELL TOWER**
                                              15893-7/$3.50

A BANTAM SKYLARK BOOK

FRANCINE PASCAL'S

SWEET VALLEY Twins AND FRIENDS

Buy them at your local bookstore or use this handy page for ordering:

Bantam Books, Dept. SVT3, 2451 S. Wolf Road, Des Plaines, IL 60018

Please send me the items I have checked above. I am enclosing $_____
(please add $2.50 to cover postage and handling). Send check or money
order, no cash or C.O.D.s please.

Mr/Ms _____

Address _____

City/State _____ Zip _____

SVT3-3/93

Please allow four to six weeks for delivery.
Prices and availability subject to change without notice.